餐飲英語

Restaurant English

蔡淳伊◎著

餐旅叢書序

餐旅叢書序

　　近年來，隨著世界經濟的發展，觀光餐飲業已成為世界最大的產業。為順應世界潮流及配合國內旅遊事業之發展，各類型具有國際水準的觀光大飯店、餐廳、咖啡廳、休閒俱樂部，如雨後春筍般建立，此一情勢必能帶動餐飲業及旅遊事業的蓬勃發展。

　　餐旅業是目前最熱門的服務業之一，面對世界性餐飲業之劇烈競爭，餐旅服務業是以服務為導向的專業，有賴大量人力之投入，服務品質之提升實是刻不容緩之重要課題。而服務品質之提升端賴透過教育途徑以培養專業人才始能克竟其功，是故餐飲教育必須在教材、師資、設備方面，加以重視與實踐。

　　餐旅服務業是一門範圍甚廣的學科，在其廣泛的研究領域中，包括顧客和餐旅管理及從業人員，兩者之間相互搭配，相輔相成，互蒙其利。然而，從業人員之訓練與培育非一蹴可幾，著眼需要，長期計畫予以培養，方能適應今後餐旅行業的發展；由於科技一日千里，電腦、通信、家電（三C）改變人類生活形態，加上實施隔週週休二日，休閒產業蓬勃發展，餐旅行業必然會更迅速成長，因而往後餐旅各行業對於人才的需求自然更殷切，導致從業人員之教育與訓練更加重要。

餐飲英語

　　餐旅業蓬勃發展，國內餐旅領域中英文書籍進口很多，中文書籍較少，並且涉及的領域明顯不足，未能滿足學術界、從業人員及消費者的需求，基於此一體認，擬編撰一套完整餐旅叢書，以與大家分享。經與揚智文化總經理葉忠賢先生構思，此套叢書應著眼餐旅事業目前的需要，作為餐旅業界往前的指標，並應能確實反應餐旅業界的真正需要，同時能使理論與實務結合，滿足餐旅類科系學生學習需要，因此本叢書將有以下幾項特點：

1. 餐旅叢書範圍著重於國際觀光旅館及休閒產業，舉凡旅館、餐廳、咖啡廳、休閒俱樂部之經營管理、行銷、硬體規劃設計、資訊管理系統、行業語文、標準作業程序等各種與餐旅事業相關內容，都在編撰之列。
2. 餐旅叢書採取理論和實務並重，內容以行業目前現況為準則，觀點多元化，只要是屬於餐旅行業的範疇，都將兼容並蓄。
3. 餐旅叢書之撰寫性質不一，部分屬於編撰者，部分屬於創作者，也有屬於授權翻譯者。
4. 餐旅叢書深入淺出，適合技職體系各級學校餐旅科系作為教科書，更適合餐旅從業人員及一般社會大眾當作參考書籍。

5.餐旅叢書為落實編撰內容的充實性與客觀性,編者帶領
　學生赴歐海外實習參觀旅行之際,搜集歐洲各國旅館大
　學教學資料,訪問著名旅館、餐廳、酒廠等,給予作者
　撰寫之參考。

6.餐旅叢書各書的作者,均獲得國內外觀光餐飲碩士學位
　以上,並在國際觀光旅館實際參與經營工作,學經歷豐
　富。

　　身為餐旅叢書的編者,謹在此感謝本叢書中各書的作者,
若非各位作者的奉獻與合作,本叢書當難以順利付梓,最後要
感謝揚智文化事業股份有限公司總經理、總編輯及工作人員支
持與工作之辛勞,才能使本叢書順利的呈現在讀者面前。

陳堯帝　謹識

中華民國八十八年八月

序

　　隨著世界地球村的發展趨勢,觀光業已成為新世紀的明星產業,台灣也正朝向成為亞太營運中心而努力,此一情勢必然帶動國內經濟及觀光餐飲事業的蓬勃發展。

　　目前國內從事觀光、餐飲業的成員接觸外國人士的機會很多,為了提升服務品質,餐飲服務人員的英語會話能力更形重要。「餐館英語」是面對不斷湧進的觀光客及日益增多的商務旅客溝通與瞭解的重要工具。為了落實觀光、餐飲英語教育,筆者特別編著此書,除了適合觀光、餐飲科系學生的學習,也可協助相關的現職從業人員練習各種實務英語會話,以面對各種不同場合所需。

　　本書編撰以實用,易懂易學為原則,深入淺出,內容豐富。相信對提高餐飲英語溝通之能力,必有所助益。本書具有下列特色:

1.本書內容共分十一章,涵蓋與餐飲相關領域所常使用的英語字彙和句型。

2.本書為便利使用者學習,編排力求簡明扼要、明確清晰。

3.本書除了有實用英語會話、句型、文法分析，並且設計
　與主題內容相關的練習題，幫助讀者測試自己的理解程
　度，同時強化演練的實用效果。

　　筆者特別要感謝長官的鼓勵、父母的栽培及家人的支持，
使本書得以順利完成。全書雖經縝密編著，疏漏之處在所難
免，尚祈各界專家先進不吝賜教。也希望本書能帶給讀者實質
有效的幫助，這也是筆者衷心的期盼。

　　　　　　　　　　　　　蔡淳伊　謹識

CONTENTS

CONTENTS

餐飲英語

CHAPTER 1

CHAPTER 1

RESERVATIONS

餐飲英語

Taking Reservations

I'd like to make a reservation.

*For which date?

*For what time?

*How many in your party?

*What's your name?

#Repeat all information

"Your reservation is for August 9th at 18:30 for 10 people, under the name Joy Smith. Is that correct?"

CONVERSATION I
Making a reservation

Host: Good afternoon, Ming Garden Restaurant. This is
       Steven. How may I help you?

Customer: I'd like to make a reservation.

Host: Certainly, Madam. For what day?

Customer: September 8th.

Host: And for what time, please?

Customer: Seven p.m.

Host: How many people will there be in your party?

Customer: There will be six.

Host: All right. Could I have your name and phone number, please?

Customer: Sure. My name is Carla Lyder and the phone number is 2210-6789.

Host: OK, Miss Lyder, that'll be a table for six at seven p.m. on September 8th. Is that correct?

Customer: Right.

Host: Thank you for calling. We look forward to seeing you.

Customer: Thank you. Goodbye.

Host: Goodbye.

USEFUL EXPRESSIONS

1. I would like to reserve a table.

   I'd like to book a table.

   I want to make a reservation.

   我想訂位。

2. I'd like to book a table for ...(number of people) on/for ...(date) at ...(time).

   我想訂位。共XXX人（人數），XXX（日期），XXX

（時間）。

3. Do you have a private room for sixteen persons?

你們有可以容納十六個人的包廂嗎？

4. How do you spell your name, please?

請問您的名字要怎麼寫？

5. Our restaurant can keep the table for you for fifteen minutes. Please arrive before 7:15 p.m.

我們餐廳能幫您保留十五分鐘的位子，請在晚上七點十五分以前到達。

6.
Could you speak a bit more | loudly / slowly |, please?

請您 | 說大聲點 / 說慢點 | 好嗎?

7. (May) I beg your pardon?

抱歉，我沒聽清楚，請再說一遍。

8. I'd like to confirm your reservation.

我想確認您的訂席。

CHAPTER 1

CONVERSATION II
Making special requests

Hostess: Good morning, MiMi's Restaurant. May I help you?

Customer: I want to book a table for three on Valentine's Day at six o'clock. We need to be at the concert by seven-thirty.

Hostess: Oh? Just a moment, please. Hello? I'm very sorry, but we don't have a table available for six o'clock.

Customer: Oh, no !

Hostess: Well, we could seat you at six-thirty though.

Customer: That would be fine. And one more thing...could we sit by the window?

Hostess: Sorry, Sir. We've run out of all the tables by the window at that time, but you might like to sit by the band.

Customer: OK. That would be fine. Thank you very much.

Hostess: You are welcome.

餐飲英語

USEFUL EXPRESSIONS

1. I'm sorry, we're fully booked.

   I'm afraid we haven't any tables left.

   Sorry, we don't have any tables available now.

   抱歉，我們已經客滿了。

2.

   I'd like to sit
   | by the window. |
   | out of doors/outside/on the patio. |
   | in the smoking/non-smoking area. |
   | near the band. |

   我想坐在
   | 靠窗 |
   | 戶外 |
   | 吸煙區／非吸煙區 |
   | 靠近樂團 |
   的位置。

3.

   Sorry, we're out of table
   | by the window. |
   | out of doors/outside. |
   | in the smoking/non-smoking section. |
   | near the band. |

CHANGE

抱歉，我們已經沒有 靠窗 / 戶外 / 吸煙區／非吸煙區 / 靠近樂團 的位子。

4. Do you have a children's menu?

　你們餐廳有供應兒童餐嗎？

5. I'd like to make a special request.

　我想有個特殊要求。

6. I'd like a table with a view.

　我想要坐在視野好的位置。

LISTENING Ⅰ

　　Listen to three people ringing the Hard Rock Café to make reservations. Write down the information each person gives.

～Reservations～				
Date	Time	Number of people	Name	Special request
1.				
2.				
3.				

餐飲英語

CONVERSATION III
Changing the reservation

Host: Hello, Chi-Chi Restaurant. May I help you?

Customer: I'd like to change my booking.

Host: Certainly, madam.

Customer: I have a reservation for nine for lunch on the day after tomorrow. But we'd like to come for dinner rather than lunch.

Host: All right. For what time?

Customer: At quarter after seven.

Host: That'll be no problem, madam. By the way, please arrive not later than seven-thirty, because we can keep the table for only fifteen minutes.

Customer: Yes, we will. Thank you. Goodbye.

Host: You're welcome. Goodbye.

USEFUL EXPRESSIONS

1. I want to cancel my reservation.
   我想取消訂位。

2.

I'd like to change my booking to | tomorrow.
| nine-thirty.
| three persons.

我想將我的訂位改成 | 明天。
| 七點三十分。
| 九個人。

3. We're going to postpone our reservation for Wednesday to Friday.

我們想把星期三的訂席改成星期五。

4. I'd rather come for dinner at seven o'clock than eight o'clock.

我想八點來吃晚餐而不想七點來。

5. We'd like to put our reservation forward to October 19th.

我想將訂席提前到十月十九日。

6. 9:15 p.m.= nine fifteen p.m.= quarter after nine p.m.

7:45 a.m.= seven forty-five a.m.=quarter to eight a.m.

晚上九點十五分＆早上七點四十五分的說法。

LISTENING II

1. Listen to five customers calling to change their booking. Write down what each customer wants.

	1	2	3	4	5
Change time	☐	☐	☐	☐	☐
Change date	☐	☐	☐	☐	☐
Change table	☐	☐	☐	☐	☐
Change number of people	☐	☐	☐	☐	☐
Cancel booking	☐	☐	☐	☐	☐

2. Then listen to the waiters replying to the customers. If the waiter can meet the request, put a tick (∨). If they cannot meet it, put a cross (✕).

ROLE PLAY

Look at the table chart of Jimmy's Restaurant. You will see that there are two private rooms for a maximum of 16 people, six tables for 4, four tables for 6, and three tables for 8. Then look at the reservations chart for Friday December 26th. You can see that some of the tables were already booked.

Take turns being A (various customers) and B (a host/hostess). Use the table chart and reservation chart of the restaurant below.

Student A: You should call to

        (a) make reservations.

        (b) change reservations.

        (c) make special requests.

Student B: You are the host or hostess in the Jimmy's Restaurant. Answer the phone and

        (a) write down the caller's reservation.

        (b) sometimes meet the requests, sometimes not.

        (c) if you cannot meet the requests, suggest alternatives.

Table Chart

Tables 1-6 are near the band for 4 presons.

Tables 7-10 are by the window for 6 presons.

Tables 11-13 are out of doors for 8 presons.

Private rooms are for 16 presons.

Tables 1-3 are in the smoking area.

Tables 4-10 are in the non-smoking area.

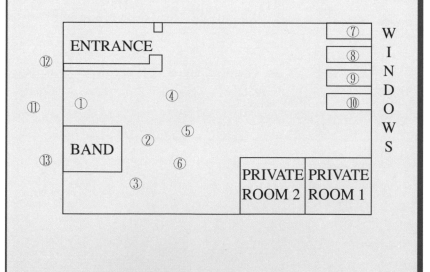

Reservations

Date_____

Lunch 11:30~14:00	Tea time 14:30~16:00	Dinner 18:00~22:30
1. _____	1. Dr. Lee 15:00 _____	1. _____
2. _____	2._____	2. _____
3. _____	3._____	3. Mr. Hamilton 18:30
4. _____	4._____	4. Mr. Smith 19:00
5. _____	5. Ms. Wang 14:30	5. Mr. Smith 19:00
6. Mr. Carter 12:00	6._____	6. _____
7. _____	7._____	7. Mrs. Spencer 20:00
8. _____	8._____	8. _____
9. Mrs. Gallway 13:20	9. Mr. Watson 14:45	9. _____
10. Mr. Kennedy 12:45	10._____	10. Mr. Pearson 18:45
11. _____	11._____	11. _____
12. _____	12._____	12. _____
13. _____	13._____	13. Ms. King 19:30
Private 1 Rotary 12:30 International	Private 1 _____	Private 1 _____
Private 2_____	Private 2 _____	Private 2 Lion's Club 19:00

FILL IN

1. You are not allowed to smoke here. This is a _____ section.

2. Do you have children's _____ for my six-year-old son to order?

3. Sorry, we cannot accept your reservation. We are fully
   _____.

4. Originally, my reservation is on May 2nd, but I want to put
   it _____ to May 8th.

5. I'd like to have a view in the restaurant, so I want to sit
   near the _____.

VOCABULARY & PHRASES

Nouns

customer/guest   request

host/hostess   table chart

Valentine's Day   reservation chart

band   children's menu

Verbs

to reserve   to postpone

to book   to put ... forward to

to confirm   to look forward to

to cancel

Prepositions

be run out of ...

CHAPTER 2

CHAPTER 2

ON THE TABLE

 餐飲英語

Look at the table settings below. Fill in the name of the tablewares in the blank.

American service table setting

1._____	7._____	13._____
2._____	8._____	14._____
3._____	9._____	15._____
4._____	10._____	16._____
5._____	11._____	
6._____	12._____	

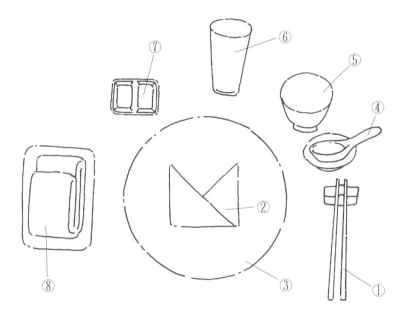

Chinese service table setting

1._____   4._____   7._____

2._____   5._____   8._____

3._____   6._____

TRUE OR FLLSE

Put a "T" by those statements that would be proper, and put a "F" by those which would be not right. Then discuss your answers with other students.

餐飲英語

1._____ The different knives and forks are for the different courses. The small knife and fork are for the main course; the big ones are for the first course.

2._____ When we serve Shao Shin wine, we pour out the wine into the Shao Shin serving glass first.

3._____ We set forks on the left, and knives (and soup spoons) on the right.

4._____ To cut out food, we usually hold the knife in the left hand and the fork in the right hand.

5._____ When we are not using the chopsticks during the meal, we rest them on the chopstick stand.

6._____ The shape/size of a fish knife is different from the shape/size of a dinner knife.

7._____ The small spoon and fork above a dinner plate are for having the dessert.

8._____ As a general rule, when we use the silverware on the table, we start from the outside part.

9._____ The red wine glass is smaller than the white wine glass.

10._____ There are usually at least two glasses on the table. They are put on the left, above the forks.

Position:

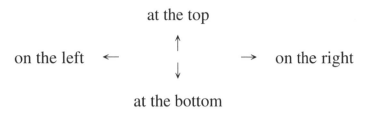

CONVERSATION

Customer 1: Excuse me. Waiter?

Waiter: Yes, sir.

Customer 1: Do you have a napkin, please?

Waiter: Don't you have one?

Customer 1: Yes, I do. But my friend doesn't.

Waiter: Oh, sorry. I'll go get one.

Customer 2: And could you bring us some water? I'm thirsty.

Waiter: Certainly. Do you need anything else?

Customer 1: Yes. Could you bring me another fork? This
one is bent.

Waiter: I'll bring you a fork right away.

Customer 2: What's this on the table?

Waiter: It's a finger bowl. It's for washing your fingers
before eating the crabs.

USEFUL EXPRESSIONS

1. Customer:

Please bring us Could I have	some	sugar. tea. soy sauce. juice. toothpicks.

OR

Could you bring me I'd like	a	tea cup. champagne tulip. salt shaker. creamer.

CHAPTER 2

顧客：

我想要 請拿給我	一些	糖。 茶。 醬油。 果汁。 牙籤。

或是

請你拿給我 我想要	一個	茶杯。 香檳杯。 鹽罐。 奶盅

2. Waiter:

Certainly, Sir/Madam.		
I'll bring you I'll get you	some fruit some butter a sugar bowl a lobster pick a bottle of wine a glass of cocktail a cup of coffee a basket of bread	immediately. right away. straightaway. at once.

服務生：

沒有問題，先生／小姐。	
我立刻拿給您	一些水果。 一些奶油。 一個糖盅。 一個龍蝦叉。 一瓶酒。 一杯雞尾酒。 一籃麵包。 一杯咖啡。

3. Customer:

Could you bring me another ... ?		
napkin		stained.
saucer		broken.
The plate	is	chipped.
knife		blunt.
fork		bent.
spoon		dirty.

顧客：

你能拿另外一條／一個／一把……給我嗎？		
這條口布		有污點的。
這個底盤		破掉了的。
這個盤子	是	有裂痕的。
這把刀子		鈍掉了的。
這把叉子		彎曲了的。
這把湯匙		髒的。

4.

The fish knife		cutting the fish.
The water jug		holding water.
The nutcracker	is for	breaking the nuts.
The corkscrew		getting out the cork.
The wine cooler		keeping the wine cool.

魚刀		切魚肉的。
水壺		裝水的。
胡桃鉗	是用來	敲開胡桃的。
開瓶器		拔軟木塞的。
冰桶		讓酒保持冰涼的。

LISTENING

1. Listen to the conversation between the customers and the waiters. Write down what each customer's problem is.

Customer 1_____

Customer 2_____

Customer 3_____

Customer 4_____

Customer 5_____

2. One family is having dinner at a restaurant. Read the statement below. Then listen to the conversation and say **True** or **False**.

   (a) The parents cleaned up the broken glass.

   (b) The waiter helped them right away.

   (c) Michael broke two glasses.

ROLE PLAY

Student A: You are the customer in a restaurant, and

        (a) you try to ask the waiter to bring something for you.

        (b) there's something wrong with the tableware.

CHAPTER 2

You complain about that and ask the waiter to change it.

Student B: You are the waiter/waitress in a restaurant. Apologize and offer to bring the items that are needed.

GRAMMAR FOCUS

1.

> We use **some** in positive statements, **any** in negative statements, and **some/any** in questions.

I'd like to have	some	salt. cream. strawberries.

Do you need	some	bowls? chopsticks?
	any	pepper? dressing?

We don't have	any	cream. tea. spoon.

2.

Countable nouns have both singular and plural forms. cup knife cups knives	Mass nouns have one form. sugar water

Could I have	a	tea spoon, chopstick,	please?
	some	tea spoons, chopsticks,	

Could I have some	butter,	please?
	juice,	

EXERCISE

Complete the conversation with **a**, **some**, and **any**.

Tina: Excuse me.

Waiter: Yes?

Tina: I don't have _____ dinner forks.

Waiter: Oh, I'm sorry. I'll go get one immediately.

Matthew: And I'd like to have _____ glass of orange juice.

Waiter: Certainly, Sir. Can I get you anything else?

Matthew: Yes. Do you have _____ suitable dessert for a
vegetarian?

*** after a few minutes ***

Tina: Waiter! Please bring me _____ dinner fork. I still
don't have one.

Matthew: And we need _____ ketchup. This bottle is
empty.

Waiter: Of course.

VOCABULARY & PHRASES

Nouns

table setting   soy sauce

tableware   Shao Shin wine

Chinaware

show plate   sauce boat

餐飲英語

dinner plate	creamer
tea cup & saucer	sugar bowl
coffee cup & saucer	toothpick holder
B & B plate	ashtray

Glassware

water glass	Irish coffee glass
wine glass	punch bowl
whisky shot	shot glass
Shao Shin serving glass	sherry & port glass
champagne tulip	

Silverware

dinner fork & knife	chopstick stand
salad fork & knife	tea/coffee spoon
dessert fork & spoon	soup ladle
fish knife & spoon	cake server
butter knife	

Other Items

napkin	coffee/tea pot
towel	finger bowl
toothpick	tray
corkscrew	tablecloth

salt & pepper shakers	service towel
chopsticks	bill holder
water jug	soup tureen
wine cooler	chafing dish

Adjectives

stained	blunt
broken	bent
chipped	

Prepositions

on the top	on the right
on the bottom	right away
on the left	

CHAPTER 3

RECEIVING CUSTOMERS AND TAKING ORDERS

Greetings

- "Good _____, welcome to _____."
- "Do you have a reservation?"
- If yes, "Let me show you to your table."
- If no, "Please wait a moment. I'll check to see if we have a table available."
- "Please follow me."
- "Here's your table. Enjoy your meal."

Service Greetings

- "Good _____, my name is _____. Please let me know if there's anything you need."
- "Here are your menus. Let me know when you're ready to order."
- "Would you like something to drink?"
- "Is there anything you need me to explain?"

What's on the Menu

- Appetizers/starters
- Soups
- Salads
- Main course
- Desserts
- Specials of the Day
- Chef's Recommendations
- Special Set-Menu

CHAPTER 3

List the order in which restaurant staff do these things.

_____ (a) Confirm the orders like this: "You ordered ..., and you wanted ...."

_____ (b) Guide guests to the table.

_____ (c) Go and get customers' orders.

_____ (d) Serve water.

_____ (e) Greet guests and verify reservation if made.

_____ (f) Ask the customers if they want anything else. (e.g., to drink, a salad, or a dessert).

_____ (g) Present the menu.

_____ (h) Ask customers what they would like and write down each person's order.

CONVERSATION I
Greeting and seating the guests

Host: Good afternoon, madam. Welcome to Dynasty Restaurant. Do you have a reservation?

Guest: No.

Host: How many persons, please?

Guest: A table for six.

餐飲英語

Host: Where would you prefer to sit?

Guest: Well, a table with a good view, please.

Host: I'll show you to your table. This way, please.

Guest: Thank you.

Host: Will this be alright for you?

Guest: Can we have that table over there?

Host: I'm afraid that table is reserved.

Guest: O.K. Then, this table is fine.

Host: Please take a seat.

Guest: Thanks.

Host: A waiter will come to take your order in just a minute.

USEFUL EXPRESSIONS

1. A table for nine.

   需要有九個人的座位。

2. Where would you like to sit?

   您希望坐哪裡？

3. This way, please.

   Please follow me.

   這邊請。

4. How about this table?

坐這裡好嗎？

5. Would you prefer a table in the main restaurant or in a private room?

您喜歡大廳的座位，還是房間的位子？

6. I need to check for it.

我需要去查詢一下。

7. I'm afraid that table is reserved.

那個位子恐怕已經被預定了。

8. Shall I bring a high chair for your child?

需要幫您的小孩拿張高腳椅嗎？

9. Your server will be with you in just one moment.

服務生立刻會過來為您服務。

CONVERSATION II
Asking the guests to wait

Hostess: Good afternoon, sir. Welcome to White Castle. Do you have a reservation?

Guest: No.

Hostess: I'm sorry, sir. All our tables are occupied at this

moment. Would you mind waiting? We'll arrange a
table for you as soon as possible.

Guest: Well, how long will it take?

Hostess: I'm not quite sure, sir. If you're in a hurry, we also
serve excellent Chinese cuisine on the second floor.

Guest: That's fine. I'll wait.

Hostess: May I have your name, please?

Guest: Yes. It's Pearson.

Hostess: Mr. Pearson, you might want to have a seat over
there and we'll call you as soon as the table is
available.

Guest: O.K. Thank you.

***   after a few minutes   ***

Hostess: Mr. Pearson, we have a table for you now. Please
follow me. We're sorry to keep you waiting. A
waiter will come to take your order in just a
minute.

USEFUL EXPRESSIONS

1. Sorry, we have no free tables now.

   Sorry, we're full at the moment.

Sorry, we're fully booked.

抱歉，我們已客滿。

2. Thank you for waiting.

Sorry for the delay.

抱歉，讓您久等了。

3. (request for waiting)

I'll be with you, shortly.

I'll be right with you.

One moment, please.

我立刻就來。

CONVERSATION III
Taking customers' orders

The Clinton family is having dinner in a restaurant.

Waiter: Good evening. Here's your menu. Please take your time. When you're ready to order, please call me.

***   after a few minutes   ***

Waiter: May I take your order now?

Mrs. Clinton: Yes, I think so.

Waiter: What would you like to start?

Mrs. Clinton: I'll have clear ox tail soup to start with.

Waiter: And what would you like to follow?

Mrs. Clinton: I'll have the rainbow trout with almond.

Waiter: Would you like any dessert? Our restaurant's having a "tropical fruit festival" now. Would you care for the fruit dessert?

Mrs. Clinton: Oh, what kind of fruit desserts do you have?

Waiter: We have pear soufflé, coconut ice cream, apricot tart ....

Mrs. Clinton: Hmm... I think I'd like the flambe cherries with kirsch. How about you, Cher?

Daughter: Uh, maybe I'll try a roast beef sandwich and a large soda. No, wait, I changed my mind. I'll have the fried chicken instead.

Waiter: O.K. Would you like a soup or salad to begin?

Daughter: Yes, I'd like a green salad.

Waiter: What kind of dressing would you like? We have Thousand Island, Italian, French, and Blue Cheese.

Daughter: Thousand Island, please.

Waiter: And what about you, sir?

Mr. Clinton: For an appetizer, I think I'll take the smoked

salmon.

Waiter: What will you have for the main course?

Mr. Clinton: I'll have the grilled beef tenderloin.

Waiter: How would you like your steak?

Mr. Clinton: Medium rare, please.

Waiter: O.K. Anything for you to drink, sir?

Mr. Clinton: Umm... a cup of hot tea.

Waiter: Then, let me repeat your orders. You just ordered one clear ox tail soup, one rainbow trout with almond, one flambe cherries with kirsch, one fried chicken with large soda, an order of medium rare sirloin steak, and a cup of hot tea. Will there be anything else?

Mr. Clinton: No, that'll be all. Thank you.

Waiter: Thank you.

USEFUL EXPRESSIONS

1. when presenting the menu:

   This is our menu, please take your time.

   I'd like to show you our set menu and a la carte menu.

   Here's the menu.

餐飲英語

上菜單時：

這是我們的菜單，請慢慢看。

這是我們套餐及單點菜單。

這是我們的菜單。

2. Do you have a vegetarian menu?

你們有素食菜單嗎？

3. May I take your order now?

Are you ready to order?

Would you like to order now?

您準備好要點餐了嗎？

4. We need a few more minutes.

我們還需要一些時間來決定要點什麼。

5. Major courses in a menu:　西式菜單中主要項目：

    appetizers/hors d'oeuvre　　　　開胃菜

    soups　　　　　　　　　　　　湯

    salads　　　　　　　　　　　　沙拉

    main courses/entrees　　　　　　主菜

    desserts　　　　　　　　　　　甜點

CHAPTER 3

6.

I'd like	the onion soup.
I'll have	scones with whipped cream.
I'll take	the broiled prawns with trout caviar.
I'll try	the French goose liver pâte with wine jelly.

	洋蔥湯。
我想點	英式鬆餅夾鮮奶油。
	魚子醬燴明蝦。
	紅酒凍法國鵝肝醬。

7. Sorry, we're out of fish.

I'm afraid the fish is all gone.

I'm afraid the fish has been sold out.

抱歉，恐怕魚已經都賣完了。

8.

Would you care for some	salad?
	soup?

想要來點	沙拉	嗎？
	湯	

9.

What kind of	dessert soup	do you have?

你們餐廳有什麼樣的	甜點？ 湯？

10. What kind of dressing would you like?

您需要哪種沙拉醬？

11. Will there be anything else?

您還要點些什麼嗎？

12.

How	do
	
	would
		you	want
			
			like
				your	steak? Rare, medium
					    or well-done?
					sandwich? White or wheat?
					coffee? Black or with
					    cream or sugar?

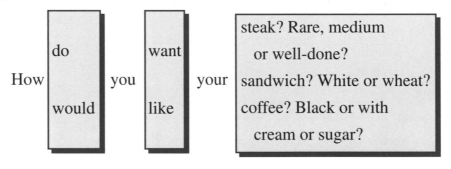

您想要什麼樣的	牛排？稍熟、五分熟、還是全熟？ 三明治？白麵包或全麥麵包？ 咖啡？黑咖啡還是加糖或奶精？

13. when ordering the steak:

I'd like I'll have	it	rare. medium rare. medium. medium well. well done.

點牛排時：

我想要	稍熟的。 三分熟的。 五分熟的。 七分熟的。 全熟的。

14. Dressing沙拉醬的種類很多，最常見的有：
Vinaigrette（油醋汁），Blue Cheese（藍乳酪醬），
Italian（義式沙拉醬），Thousand Island（千島沙拉醬），French（法式沙拉醬）。

15. 在與食物的搭配上，常使用的醬料有：
Mayonnaise（美乃滋；蛋黃醬），Tartare Sauce（塔塔醬），Chili Sauce（辣椒醬），Tabasco Sauce（辣醬

油），Ketchup（蕃茄醬），Horseradish Sauce（辣根醬；芥茉醬）。

EXERCISE

Complete the chart with words from the list. What's your favorite food in each category?

Appetizers	Soups	Salads	Entrees	Desserts
_____	_____	_____	_____	_____
_____	_____	_____	_____	_____

frozen yogurt   roast whole baby chicken

beef consomme   pickled jellyfish

rib eye steak   roast rack of lamb

creamy asparagus soup   spicy chicken salad

seafood chowder   baked snail

tuna fish salad   cherry pie

banana split   smoked salmon

chef's salad

CHAPTER 3

LISTENING I

A. Listen and check (∨) the best response.

1. ☐ French, please.
   ☐ I'll have a soup.

2. ☐ Yes, I will.
   ☐ Cheese cake, please.

3. ☐ Yes, this way, please.
   ☐ No, we haven't decided yet.

4. ☐ No, I don't think so.
   ☐ I'd like it medium.

5. ☐ No, he doesn't.
   ☐ Yes, I'll have coffee, please.

6. ☐ We need a few more minutes.
   ☐ Thank you. I'll take one.

B. Listen to each conversation. Then write **"That's right"** or **"That's wrong"** after each statement.

Sweet Home Restaurant

Soups		Desserts	
Cream of mushroom soup	$150	Ice cream	$40
Vegetable soup	95	Cherry pie	55
Salads		Beverages	
Green salad	$65	Coffee or tea	$40
Chicken salad	105	Soda	35
		Beer	50

Pasta

Spaghetti with meatballs	$170
Lasagna	130

Dinner Special

Lamb chops

Roast beef

Fried chicken

$350

All dinner specials

served with choice of

potato (mashed, baked, or

French fries), soup or salad.

1. She wants spaghetti with seafood. _____

2. He orders soda as a drink. _____

3. The waiter is going to bring her some coffee now. _____

4. He likes mashed potatoes. _____

5. He doesn't want any soup. _____

6. He's not ready to order yet. _____

CONVERSATION IV
Recommending dishes

There are a woman and a man having lunch in a restaurant. Alice is their waitress.

Alice: Good afternoon, my name's Alice, and I'll be taking care of your table. If there's anything you need, please call me. I'll be glad to help.

Man: Thank you.

Alice: Are you ready to order?

Woman: Yes, I'd like a mixed garden salad to start with. But I haven't decided about a soup. I'm on a diet. Can you recommend something for me?

Alice: Certainly, madam. Our Italian vegetable soup made

with fresh celery, asparagus, carrots, and beans is low in calories. It's light and suitable for you.

Woman: O.K. I'll take it. I'm still wondering about my dessert.

Alice: Why don't you try the low fat frozen yogurt? It's on top of a fruit cocktail. I'm sure you'll enjoy it.

Woman: It sounds good. I'll try it.

Alice: And what about you, sir?

Man: What would you suggest as an appetizer?

Alice: If I were you, I'd try the duck liver pâte. It's very tasty.

Man: Good. I'll try one.

Alice: Would you like seafood or meat as your main course?

Man: I prefer seafood.

Alice: The grilled king prawns, pan fried fillet of trouts, and sauteed scallops in our restaurant are very popular. Especially the king prawns, they are in season at the moment and are very good.

Man: Grilled king prawns sounds good. I'll have that.

Alice: And would you like anything to drink? I would suggest a dry white wine to go with your prawns.

Man: All right. I'll have a glass of white wine.

　　有時客人不確定所要點的菜餚時，服務生可適時的幫客人推薦餐點。

　　但在推薦之前必須先瞭解到不同客人的喜好與需求，然後再針對個人飲食上的特點推薦出真正符合其需求的菜餚。例如：有人對食物口味上有其酸、甜、鹹、辣（sour, sweet, salty, spicy）上不同的喜好。還有因宗教信仰上的因素，而使得回教徒（Muslim）不能吃豬肉（pork），豬肉加工品如：火腿、培根、香腸（ham, bacon, sausage），甲殼類海產（shellfish），例如：蝦、蟹（shrimp, crab）、鰻魚（eels），以及酒精（alcohol）等食物的禁忌。對於Jew（猶太教信徒）而言，他們在飲食上亦有所禁忌。凡是豬肉、鰻魚、甲殼類海產、無鰭無鱗片的魚（fish without fins or scales）都是不被允許的。 而且所食之肉類及食器也都必須在符合猶太戒律的情形之下方可食用（kosher food）。吃所謂「半素」的人（vegetarian），不能食用肉類（meat）及魚類（fish）；吃「全素」者（vegan），甚至連蛋類（eggs）及乳製品（dairy products）都不可碰觸。而有些人則是因為身體上的某些需求或疾病，所以在飲食的選擇上也必須更謹慎，例如老年人（senior citizens）應考慮其食物的易咀嚼及易消化性（easy to chew and digest）；至於目前正在節食減肥的人（dieter），也要注意推薦他們低脂（low fat）或低卡（low calories）的菜餚。

餐飲英語

USEFUL EXPRESSIONS

1.

I can't make up my mind I can't decide I'm wondering	about	an appetizer. a soup. a salad. a dessert.
What would you recommend What do you suggest	as	

我還不能決定要點什麼樣的 我還在考慮要點什麼樣的	開胃菜。 湯。 沙拉。 甜點。	（嗎）？
你能幫我推薦		

2. Are you on a special diet?

   您在飲食上有特殊需求嗎？

3. Are you in a hurry?

   您有趕時間嗎？

4. If you're in a hurry, I'd recommend the pasta or fried rice.

   如果您趕時間的話，我建議您可以點麵食類或炒飯。

5. I'm afraid this dish will take about twenty minutes to

prepare, sir. Do you mind waiting?

先生，那道菜恐怕要花二十分鐘來烹調，您介不介意等一下？

6. Which flavor would you like?

   您比較喜歡哪種口味？

7. I'd suggest that you order a set course for eight persons.

   我建議您可以點八人份的合菜。

8.

I can recommend	It's They're	today's special.
		popular.
		delicious.
		excellent.
		suitable for you.
		one of chef's specialities.

我向您推薦……	因為這道菜 因為這幾道菜	是今日特餐。
		很受歡迎。
		很美味可口。
		很棒。
		很適合您。
		是主廚的拿手好菜之一。

餐飲英語

9. Would you like to try?

您要不要嚐嚐看？

10.

I'd suggest a(n) | Beaujolais / earl grey tea / cappucino | to go with the | tortellini. / bread pudding. / tiramisu.

我建議您點 | 薄酒來 / 伯爵茶 / 義大利奶泡咖啡 | 來搭配 | 義大利肉餃。/ 麵包布丁。/ 義大利乳酪蛋糕。

11.

Which is | sweeter / more expensive / richer | ?

| Chocolate sundae / Grilled lamb chops / Manhattan clam chowder | or | apple pie a la mode / lobster gratin / baked mushroom soup with puff pastry | ?

哪一種比較 | 甜 / 貴 / 香濃 | ？

巧克力聖代		蘋果派冰淇淋	
炭烤羊排	或	焗烤龍蝦	？
曼哈頓蛤蜊濃湯		酥皮蘑菇濃湯	

12.
Apple pie a la mode		sweeter	
Grilled lamb chops	is	more expensive	

	chocolate sundae.
than	lobster gratin.

OR

The Manhattan clam chowder is not | as rich as | baked mushroom soup with puff pastry.

蘋果派冰淇淋		巧克力聖代		甜。
炭烤羊排	比	焗烤龍蝦	還要	貴。

或

曼哈頓蛤蜊濃湯 | 沒有像 | 酥皮蘑菇濃湯 | 那麼香濃 | 。

13. Is it possible to have French fries instead of baked potato with the veal?

我可以不要烤馬鈴薯，而選擇薯條來搭配犢牛肉嗎？

餐飲英語

14. I'll have something hot to start with.

我開胃菜想點些帶有辣味的。

15. I'd like fish as a starter.

我開胃菜想點魚。

16. I'd like something light as a main course.

我主菜想點些口味清淡的食物。

17. I've got a large appetite. I'll have something really filling as a main course.

我的胃口很好，所以主菜想點些真正能吃飽的。

18. — If I were you, I'd try the oyster. They're excellent at this time of year.

— If I were you, I'd have the shrimp cocktail. It's very light.

— If I were you, I'd try the pan fried sole. It's one of the chef's specialities.

— If I were you, I'd try the vegetable. It's a local dish.

— 如果我是您，我會點生蠔，因為它們現在是一年當中最鮮美的時候。

— 如果我是您，我會點蝦子，因為它們很清淡。

— 如果我是您，我會點乾煎鰈魚，因為它們是主廚招牌菜之一。

— 如果我是您，我會點野菜，因為它們是當地特產。

ROLE PLAY

Work in pairs. Take turns to be **A** (a customer) and **B** (a waiter/waitress).

Use the menu on "Listening I" to practice:

(a) receiving & seating the customers.

(b) making recommendation about dishes.

to the following customers who are:

— in a hurry.

— allergic to seafood.

— senior citizen.

— on a diet.

— Muslim.

EXERCISE

Complete the conversation, using the sentences in the box.

> • We'll have chicken soup.
> • Iced coffee, I guess.
> • Would you like soup or salad with that?
> • Oh, that's mine.
> • Yes. I'd suggest the black forest cake.
> • What about you, sir?
> • How would you like your steak?
> • Could I have some melon?
> • Orange and grapefruit.
> • Certainly.

1. Waiter: Would you care for some dessert?

   Customer: I haven't decided yet. What do you suggest as a dessert?

   Waiter: _____

   Customer: All right. I'll have one.

2. Man: _____

   Waitress: O.K. Two bowls of chicken soup. Anything else to drink?

   Man: _____

   Woman: And I'll have a coke.

3. Woman: I'll have the baked snail to start with.

   Waiter: _____

   Man: I'll try the egg roll.

4. Woman: What kind of Juice do you have?

   Waiter: _____

   Woman: I'll try grapefruit.

5. Waitress: What will you order for the main course?

   Man: I'd like a grilled chicken sandwich.

   Waitress: _____

   Man: Soup, please.

LISTENING II

According the following menu.

Listen and write down what Amy and Tony order.

	Amy	Tony
Appetizers		
Soups		
Entrees		
Desserts		
Beverages		

Menu

Appetizer		Vegetables	
Barbecued suckling pig	$150	Fried fresh bamboo and pea shoots	$120
Drunken chicken	165	Pan fried vegetable with gingko	135
Cold meat combination	230	Fried seasonal vegetable	90

Soups		Rice & noodle	
Shark's fin soup	$200	Home style fried rice noodle	$180
Vegetable soup	105	Fried rice with salmon	200
Hot & sour soup	80	Vegetable noodle	145

Seafood		Desserts	
Abalone with oyster sauce	$200	Almond beancurd jelly	$60
Braised sea cucumber	210	Mango pudding	60
Pan fried scallops with fried		Sweetened sago with coconut milk	55
prawns	195	Baked egg yolk puff	70

Beef, Pork & Chicken		Beverages	
Braised pig knuckle	$225	Oolong tea	$90
Kungpao chicken	195	Jasmine tea	90
Fried beef with green pepper	225	Shao Shin wine/bottle	150

GRAMMAR FOCUS

Modal verbs would and will for requests	
What would you like to eat?	I'd like a sandwich.
	I'll have a tuna fish salad.
What kind of potato would you like?	I'd like mashed potato.
	I'll have French fries.
What would you like to drink?	I'd like a small coke.
	I'll have iced tea.

Complete this conversations. Then practice with a partner.

Waitress: What _____ you like to order?

Guest: I _____ have the rib eye steak.

Waitress: _____ you like rice or potatoes?

Guest: Rice, please.

Waitress: _____ you like a salad to start with?

Guest: Yes, I _____ have a garden salad.

Waitress: What kind of dressing _____ you like? Italian, Thousand Island, or French?

Guest: I _____ like French.

餐飲英語

Waitress: O.K. And what will _____ for drink?

Guest: No, that _____ be all for now, thanks.

VOCABULARY & PHRASES

<u>Nouns</u>

clam chowder

pork rib

(peach) pie

(cheese) cake

bread pudding

(turkey) sandwich

fried chicken

(Thousand Island) dressing

(smoked) salmon

sirloin steak

appetizer/hors d'oeuvre

onion soup

entree/main course

dessert

beverage

(beef) noodle

almond

bean curd

mango

coconut milk

egg yolk

oolong tea

jasmine tea

Shao Shin wine

green pepper

pig knuckle

sea cucumber

abalone

oyster sauce

scallop

gingko

bamboo

(rainbow) trout

(black) coffee

wheat bread

shark's fin

asparagus

jellyfish

snail

tuna fish

goose liver pate

seafood

lamb chops

spaghetti

meatball

lasagna

(strawberry) mousse

prawn

eel

alcohol

dairy products

fried rice

today's special

tenderloin steak

tartare sauce

mayonnaise

ketchup

horseradish sauce

caviar

chili sauce

tabasco sauce

baby chicken

consomme

mashed potato

celery

Beaujolais

lobster gratin

chocolate sundae

rib eye steak

apricot

flambe cherries with kirsch

a la carte menu

high chair

vegetarian

Cappuccino

earl grey tea

tiramisu

lobster

suckling pig

rice noodle

Muslim

senior citizen

low fat

low calories

recommendation

Jew

Adjective

rare

medium

well done

pickled

spicy

be suitable for ...

light

sour

delicious

excellent

rich

be allergic to ...

be on a diet

Verbs

to take an order

to greet

to take your time

to recommend

to suggest

to go with ...

to chew

to digest

to make up one's mind

to verify

to occupy

CHAPTER 4

CHAPTER 4

EXPLAINING DISHES

 餐飲英語

Look at the pictures. Use the words in the list below to identify The methods of cooking shown in each one.

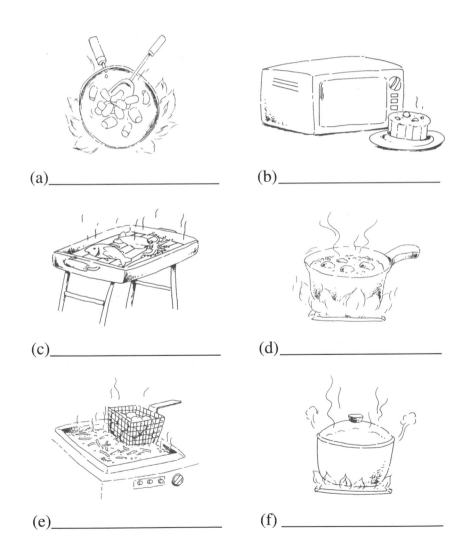

(a)_____

(b)_____

(c)_____

(d)_____

(e)_____

(f) _____

to deep fry   to bake   to boil

to grill/broil   to steam   to stir fry

EXERCISE

Circle the word that doesn't belong to each line.

(a) coconut, kiwi, pea, star fruit, honeydew melon

(b) corn, pear, cauliflower, green pepper, spinach

(c) yogurt, cheese, milk, honey, cream

(d) parsley, basil, rosemary, mint, mushroom

(e) caviar, liver, kidney, heart, tongue

(f) cuttlefish, scallop, veal, clam, sea bass

(g) pistachio, walnut, almond, raisin, peanut

CONVERSATION I

Guest: Good afternoon.

Waiter: Good afternoon, madam. May I take your order?

Guest: Yes, I'd like the plaice. How's it done?

Waiter: It's a fried fillet of plaice, madam. It's dipped in
         beaten egg, covered with breadcrumbs and then

fried. It's served with a piece of lemon and tartare sauce.

Guest: I'll have that.

Waiter: Would you like an appetizer or soup to start?

Guest: Oh, yes. Let's see ... what's the soup of the day?

Waiter: Today we have lobster bisque-a thick lobster cream soup garnished with asparagus.

Guest: Good. OK, I'll have that.

Waiter: And would you like a sweet, madam?

Guest: Yes, but not too filling. What do you suggest?

Waiter: Caramelized custard, perhaps?

Guest: No, not that. I'll have the lemon sherbet.

Waiter: All right. And would you like coffee afterwards?

Guest: Yes, please.

Waiter: Thank you, madam.

CONVERSATION II

Waitress: Good evening, sir. What would you like tonight?

Guest: Can you tell me what a Waldorf salad is?

CHAPTER 4

Waiter: Yes, it's a salad of apples, celery, and walnuts with a creamy dressing.

Guest: Oh, right, well, I'll have that first.

Waitress: And what would you like to follow?

Guest: What's chicken cacciatore?

Waitress: It's an Italian dish. It consists of chicken legs, chopped onions, sliced green peppers, canned tomatoes, and mushrooms.

Guest: Does it contain any garlic?

Waitress: Yes, it contains a little garlic.

Guest: Is there anything to go with it?

Waitress: Yes, it comes with steamed rice.

Guest: It sounds good. I'll try that, then.

Waitress: Would you like anything to drink?

Guest: A rosé. A rosé de Provence, I think.

Waitress: That's one chicken cacciatore, one salad and a rosé.

Guest: That's it, thank you.

USEFUL EXPRESSIONS

1. ways of cutting & processing. 切割與調製程序：

to fillet（指肉、魚類，片下來）the sardines

to slice（切片）the cucumber

to mash（搗碎成泥狀）the taro

to stuff（填塞）the green pepper

to peel（剝皮）the corn

to marinate（浸泡滷汁）the chicken with spicy sauce

to mix（混和）milk and tea

to chop（剁碎）the pork

to mince（絞碎）the beef

to grate（刨絲）the carrot

to dice/cube（切丁）the ham

to beat（打）the egg white

2. condiments/seasonings 調味品：

curry（咖哩）, ginger（薑）, mustard（芥末）,

soy sauce（醬油）, vinegar（醋）, salt（鹽）,

pepper（胡椒）, nutmeg（荳蔻）, olive oil（橄欖油）,

garlic（蒜）。

3. ways of cooking 其他烹調方式的說法：

to saute（清油炒）the sole

to poach（水煮，低於 100℃）the seafood

to pan fry（平鍋煎）the prawns

to roast（指肉類，在烤箱中烤）the lamb chop

to stew（燉）the beef

4.

Customer:

> What' ...?
>
> What's this dish here?
>
> Can you tell me about this?

Waiter:

> It's a sort of ....
>
> It consists of ... and ....
>
> It's made from ....
>
> It contains ....

顧客：

> 這是道什麼菜？

服務生：

> 它是一種……。
>
> 這道菜是由……和……做成的。
>
> 這道菜裡面有放……和……。

5. Customer: Does it contain any onion/garlic/black pepper ?

Waiter: Yes. It contains ... onion.

OR

餐飲英語

No. It contains no onion/garlic/black pepper.

顧客：這道菜裡面有放洋蔥／蒜頭／黑胡椒嗎？

服務生：有的，這道菜裡面有放洋蔥／蒜頭／黑胡椒。

或者

服務生：沒有，這道菜裡面沒有放洋蔥／蒜頭／黑胡椒。

6.

Customer:

> What's it served with?
>
> What does it come with?
>
> Is there anything to go with it?
>
> Does it come with rice?

Waiter:

> No, it's served on its own.
> Yes, it comes with ....
> Yes, it's served with ....

顧客：

> 這道菜有附任何東西嗎？
> 這道菜有附米飯嗎？

服務生：

> 沒有，這道菜沒有任何附餐。
> 有的，這道菜有附……。

7. — The cod is sauteed in butter and served with bearnaise sauce and Dijon mustard.

— The mussels are cooked in a white wine sauce.

— The king prawns are grilled and served with mint sauce and vegetable.

— The U.S. beef tenderloin is accompanied with oyster.

— Grilled items are garnished with a choice of mixed vegetables, French fries, potato gratin.

— This green pepper is stuffed with ground pork.

— This salad is made from romaine lettuce and smoked chicken breast.

— This veal is flavored with Provence herbs.

— This pancake is filled with whipped cream.

— 這塊鱈魚在奶油裡煎，並附有奶油蛋黃醬及法國第戎芥茉醬。

— 這道貽貝是在白酒中烹煮。

— 這份明蝦是用烤的，而且附有薄荷醬及時蔬。

— 這塊菲力牛排有附鮮蠔。

— 所有鐵扒項目皆搭配自選時蔬、炸薯條或焗烤洋芋。

— 這青椒填塞滿了絞碎的豬肉。

— 這道沙拉是由羅蔓生菜及煙燻雞胸肉做成的。

— 這道犢牛肉用香料來調味。

— 這塊煎餅裏面夾有鮮奶油。

WORK IN PAIRS

How do things taste? Discuss how you think the ingredients, dishes or sauces that you can describe with the words in the list.

Spicy (hot) : chili, pepper,

Creamy (rich):

Plain (bland):

Greasy:

Sweet:

Salty:

Sour: lemon,

Bitter: strong coffee,

EXERCISE

Which verb or verbs can you use before each of the nouns?

ex. chop the cabbage

1. mince   the potato

2. peel   the water

3. pour   the beef

4. boil   the cookies

5. mix   the coffee

6. bake   the butter and sugar

LISTENING I

Listen to people describing how to make the things below.
Try to find out what they are.

mixed green salad

pizza

_____

_____

popcorn

fried rice

_____

_____

DESCRIBING A PROCESS

How do you make it?					
First, Then, Next, After that,	chop up boil fry steam cook add	the chicken. the eggplant. shrimp. dumplings. the turkey. the avocado.			
Finally,	put pour place	the rice the sauce	into	a bowl a dish a plate	and serve.

A: Your cake was delicious. Can you tell me the recipe?

B: Sure. <u>First</u>, mix together a cup of flour, a teaspoon of salt, and two tablespoons of water.

A: I see.

B: <u>Then</u>, add half a cup of sugar. Are you with me so far?

A: Yes. I'm following you.

B: Okay. <u>Next</u>, add two eggs.

A: Uh-huh.

B: And <u>after that</u>, put the mixture into a baking pan and bake for one hour at 350 degrees. Have you got all that?

A: Yes, I've got it. Thanks.

The instructions for the following recipes are all mixed up! Put the instructions in the correct order. (by using First, Then, Next, After that, Finally).

Sure, _____ bake it for one and a half hours at 350 degrees.

   <u>First,</u> put salt, pepper, and garlic all over the roast.

_____ put it on a rack in the oven.

_____ serve it with baked potatoes and a salad.

Certainly, _____ add bean sprouts and green beans and cook
the mixture for three minutes.

_____ boil the noodles for three minutes.

_____ stir in soy sauce and sesame seeds and serve.

_____ fry pork, ginger, and garlic for five minutes.

_____ add noodles and fry for two minutes.

CHAPTER 4

ROLE PLAY

Think about dishes you know - starters, main courses and desserts.

How can you describe them to a guest?

Take it in turns to play the roles of a CUSTOMER and a WAITER/WAITRESS.

WAITER/WAITRESS: Show your menu to the customer.

CUSTOMER: Ask about each of the dishes on the menu.

WAITER/WAITRESS: Explain how each dish is cooked.

餐飲英語

LISTENING II

We asked three people the questions below. Listen and put a check (∨) next to their answers.

	Person 1	Person 2	Person 3
What's it?	☐It's a kind of soup. ☐It's a vegetable dish. ☐It's a one-pot dish.	☐It's a kind of stew. ☐It's a vegetable dish. ☐It's a kind of pasta.	☐It's a kind of soup. ☐It's an appetizer. ☐It's a dessert.
What's it made of?	☐Beef ☐Vegetables ☐Fish ☐Noodles	☐potatoes ☐onions ☐sausage ☐ground beef	☐onions ☐milk ☐apples ☐eggs
How's it cooked?	☐It's simmered. ☐It's fried. ☐It's broiled	☐It's boiled. ☐It's fried. ☐It's baked.	☐It's fried. ☐It's baked. ☐It doesn't have to be cooked.
What does it taste like?	☐It's very spicy. ☐It's a little sweet. ☐It's bitter.	☐It's spicy. ☐It's mild. ☐It's delicious.	☐It's sour. ☐It's sweet. ☐It's salty.

CHAPTER 4

VOCABULARY & PHRASES

Nouns

kiwi	teaspoon
star fruit	recipe
honeydew melon	ginger
cauliflower	soy sauce
spinach	vinegar
parsley	olive oil
basil	cod
rosemary	mussel
mint	popcorn
liver	plaice
kidney	breadcrumb
tongue	bisque
cuttlefish	sherbet
sea bass	pistachio
avocado	raisin
dumpling	peanut
eggplant	pear
tablespoon	

餐飲英語

Verbs

to grill/broil	to slice
to steam	to mash
to boil	to dice/cube
to poach	to peel
to bake	to stuff
to deep fry	to mince
to pan fry	to grate
to pour	to beat
to roast	to mix
to stew	to marinate
to fillet	to dip
to chop	

Adjective

be garnished with ...	be made from ...
be served with ...	be cooked in ...
be accompanied with ...	plain/bland
be flavored with ...	bitter
be stuffed with ...	greasy

CHAPTER 5

CHAPTER 5

DURING THE MEAL

Have you eaten out at a restaurant recently? How was it? Read the restaurant review. Then answer the questions.

Last Saturday we tried Red Roof Restaurant. We found delicious food, a relaxing atmosphere, and reasonable prices. I had mixed seafood grill and my friend had the beef submarine with cole slaw and baked potato.

The seafood was excellent, and the submarine tasted good. For dessert, I had a wonderful piece of cheese cake.

Unfortunately, the service was a problem. It was slow, there weren't any spoons on our table, and the waiter didn't bring water until we asked. The coffee was not hot enough, and the waiter was too busy to give us another cup.

As I said, the food was good, but try Red Roof Restaurant for a meal when you have patience.

1. What did the writer and her friend order at Red Roof?

_____

2. What did she think of the seafood?

_____

3. What was wrong with their coffee?

_____

4. What are some good things about the restaurant?

_____

5. How was the service in Red Roof?

_____

CONVERSATION I

A young couple took their three-year-old son to a restaurant.

Hostess: Good evening. Table for three? I'll show you to your table. This way, please. Would you like a high chair for your son?

Man: Yes, thank you.

*　　　*　　　*

Waiter: Here's the ravioli with smoked salmon, sir. Please enjoy it.

Man: Thank you. How's your sauteed chicken, Susan?

Woman: It's very tender and tasty, and the vegetables were cooked just right. How do you like your ravioli?

Man: I haven't tried it yet, but it looks great and smells delicious.

Waiter: Would you like some more butter for your rolls?

Man: Sure, thank you.

Woman: Oh, no! David spills his orange juice all over the table.

Waiter: That's all right, madam. I'll clean it right away.

Woman: Thank you so much.

(After they finish their meal)

Waiter: Excuse me. May I take these plates away?

Man: Yes, please.

Waiter: Here's your fruit platter, madam. And this is your coffee, sir.

Woman: Thank you. Umm ... these fruits are juicy and sweet.

Man: My coffee is great, too. Just the way I like it: black and strong.

*　　　*　　　*

Waiter: Is everything all right with your meals?

CHAPTER 5

Man: Yes, we are really enjoying them. And your service is very good.

Waiter: Thank you. I'm glad you like them. And it's my pleasure to serve you all.

USEFUL EXPRESSIONS

1.

| It's
They're | great.
good.
delicious.
excellent. |

| 這道菜
這幾道菜 | 非常 | 好吃。
美味可口。
棒。 |

2.

| This | oyster
grilled steak
watermelon
honey glazed ham
fried chicken | is really | fresh.
tender.
juicy/sweet.
tasty.
crispy. |

 餐飲英語

| 這道 | 生蠔
炭烤牛排
西瓜
蜜汁火腿
炸雞 | 實在是很 | 新鮮。
柔嫩。
多汁／甜。
可口。
香脆。 |

3.

This is the best I've ever had.

這是我吃過最好吃的 。

4. Compliments and responses 應對恭維對答詞

   (a) Guest: Your service is excellent.

       Waiter: It's our pleasure to serve you.

       OR

       Waiter: It's been a pleasure serving you.

   (b) Guest: Thank you. That was an excellent meal.

       Waitress: Thank you. I'll be sure to tell our chef.

   (c) Guest: Your atmosphere is very good.

       Waiter: Thank you. I'll be sure to tell our manager.

(a) 客人：你們的服務好極了。

　　服務人員：為您服務是我們的榮幸。

(b) 客人：你們的菜很好吃。

　　服務人員：謝謝，我會轉告廚師的。

(c) 客人：你們餐廳氣氛很好。

　　服務人員：謝謝，我會告訴我們經理的。

5.

Would you like	some more	olives?
		soy sauce?
		coffee?
	another	roll?

您還需要再	一些	橄欖	嗎?
		醬油	
		咖啡	
	一個	餐包	

6. before cleaning tables

Excuse me. Have you finished, sir?

Excuse me. Are you finished with this, sir?

Excuse me. May I take this plate away?

要幫客人清理桌面時：

抱歉，請問您用好了嗎？

抱歉，我來幫您清理一下桌面。

7.

Would you like	some	parmesan cheese croutons ketchup tartare sauce mustard	to go with your	spaghetti. soup. French fries. fried shrimp. hamburger.

請問您要一些		義大利乾酪 麵包丁 番茄醬 塔塔醬 芥末醬	來搭配您的	義大利麵嗎？ 湯嗎？ 薯條嗎？ 炸蝦嗎？ 漢堡嗎？

CHAPTER 5

LISTENING I

We asked three people from Taipei to recommend a good restaurant. Listen and write their answers in the chart below.

	Vivian	Jim	Sophie
A. What's a good restaurant in Taipei?	Saukura's	Fisherman's House	Corner Café
B. What kind of food does it serve?	_____	_____	_____
C. What's the ambience like?	_____	_____	_____
D. How's the service?	_____	_____	_____
E. How are the prices?	_____	_____	_____

Which of the three restaurant sounds the most interesting to you? Would you like to go there? Why or why not? Tell your classmates.

PAIR WORK

What's a good restaurant in your area? Ask your partner the questions below and record his or her answers.

餐飲英語

Your partner's answers

(a) What's your favorite place to eat?_____

(b) Where is it?_____

(c) What kind of food does it serve? _____

(d) What's the ambience like? _____

(e) How's the service?_____

(f) How are the prices?_____

(g) How often do you go there? _____

(h) What do you usually order? _____

(i) What kind of dish would you recommend?_____

(j) What do you like best about this place? _____

CONVERSATION II

Tim and Frank are having lunch at a restaurant.

Tim: It has been twenty minutes since we ordered, hasn't it?

Frank: Yes, it has. Let's ask the waiter. Waiter!

Waiter: Yes, sir.

Frank: We ordered at least twenty minutes ago, but the dish still hasn't come yet.

CHAPTER 5

Waiter: I'm sorry. I'll check on your order immediately.

Frank: Please do and make it quick.

(The waiter brings the meals.)

Waiter: Your meal, sir. We're sorry for the delay. Please enjoy your meal.

*   *   *

Tim: Excuse me.

Waiter: Yes?

Tim: This is not what I ordered.

Waiter: I'm very sorry, sir. What did you order?

Tim: I ordered curry chicken not curry beef.

Waiter: I'm sorry for the mistake. I'll go change your meal at once.

*   *   *

Tim: Are you enjoying your fried rice with salmon?

Frank: The rice doesn't taste right to me. And the salmon is bad. It tastes terrible. How's your chicken?

Tim: The chicken was undercooked. I think I'll call the waiter. Excuse me, waiter.

Waiter: Yes, sir.

Tim: I think the chicken wasn't cooked enough.

Frank: And there's something wrong with my fried rice and salmon.

Waiter: I'm terribly sorry, sir. I'll take them back to the kitchen.

USEFUL EXPRESSIONS

1.

The	rib eye steak linguine fried noodles sour and spicy soup sauce	is too (are)	tough. salty. greasy. sour. spicy.

這道	肋眼牛排 扁平通心粉 炒麵 酸辣湯 醬汁	太	硬。 鹹。 油膩。 酸。 辣。

CHAPTER 5

2.

The
| vegetable |
| pork |
| wine |
| pan fried chicken with truffle |
| milk |
| grilled T-bone steak |
| toast |
| squid |

is
| overcooked/overdone. |
| undercooked/underdone. |
| stale. |
| tasteless. |
| off. |
| dry. |
| burnt. |
| spoiled. |

這
| 蔬菜 |
| 豬肉 |
| 酒 |
| 香煎雞肉鑲松露 |
| 牛奶 |
| 碳烤丁骨牛排 |
| 土司 |
| 烏賊 |

是
| 煮過熟了。 |
| 沒煮熟的。 |
| 走味了的。 |
| 沒什麼味道的。 |
| 壞掉了的。 |
| 乾澀的。 |
| 烤焦了的。 |
| 腐敗了的。 |

3.

The
| oyster |
| banana |
| star fruit |
is not
| fresh |
| ripe |
| sweet |
enough.

餐飲英語

這 | 牡蠣 / 香蕉 / 蛋糕 | 不夠 | 新鮮 / 熟 / 甜 | 。

4. This dish tastes | terrible. / horrible. / revolting.

這道菜嚐起來 | 很可怕。 / 很糟糕。 / 令人作嘔。

5. This carp tastes fishy.
   這道鯉魚嚐起來有魚腥味。

6. I don't think this is grape flavor.
   我想這不是葡萄口味的。

7. This tastes like blueberry to me.
   吃起來像葡萄口味的。

8. I think you might have given me the wrong dish.
   我想你們可能送錯菜了。

9. This seems well done, not medium.

這好像是全熟而不是五分熟。

10. When apologizing to the customer:

I'm very sorry, sir.

I'm terribly sorry, madam.

I apologize, madam.

I'm sorry about that, sir.

與客人致歉時用語：

我非常抱歉。

我為……而感到抱歉。

11. Customer: Your service is too slow.

Waiter: I'm sorry you've been inconvenienced. We'll improve it.

客人：你們的服務太慢了。

服務人員：抱歉，造成您們的不便，我們會改善的。

12. Please wait a moment, sir/madam. I'll call the manager to help you.

請您稍等，我去請經理來。

LISTENING II

Listen to the following conversation. Decide whether each customer has a "praise" or "complaint" about the

food and service. Tick (∨) the appropriate box and write down each customer's reason.

	Praise	Complaint
Customer 1	☐	☐
Customer 2	☐	☐
Customer 3	☐	☐
Customer 4	☐	☐
Customer 5	☐	☐

PAIR WORK

Take turns asking and answering the questions below. Record your partner's answers.

CHAPTER 5

Questionnaire: Eating Out

a. When was the last time
you ate out?
☐ last week ☐ three weeks ago
☐ two weeks ago ☐ more than a month ago

b. Where did you go? _____

c. How did you find out
about this place?
☐ from a friend ☐ from a sign in front
☐ from an advertisement ☐ other:

d. What kind of food does
it serve?
☐ Chinese ☐ Italian ☐ fast food
☐ Japanese ☐ other:

e. What was the ambience
like?
☐ quiet and romantic ☐ informal ☐ fancy
☐ crowded and loud ☐ exotic:

f. How was the service?
☐ friendly ☐ gracious ☐ slow
☐ polite ☐ fast

g. How were the prices?
☐ very epensive ☐ expensive
☐ average ☐ cheap

h. How was the food?
☐ excellent ☐ pretty good
☐ so-so ☐ disappointing

餐飲英語

VOCABULARY & PHRASES

<u>Nouns</u>

atmosphere	T-bone steak
submarine	truffle
patience	squid
oyster	sign
watermelon	advertisement
ambience	parmesan cheese
guidebook	crouton
ravioli	

<u>Adjectives</u>

reasonable	fresh
tender	ripe
tasty	terrible
juicy	horrible
tough	awful
salty	revolting
overcooked/overdone	spoiled
undercooked/underdone	disappointing
stale	average

CHAPTER 5

tasteless   flat

off   fishy

burnt   gracious

<u>Verbs</u>

to enjoy   to praise

to apologize   to complain

to eat out   to improve

CHAPTER 6

CHAPTER 6

ETHNIC CUISINE

餐飲英語

Match the foods to the numbers on the map.

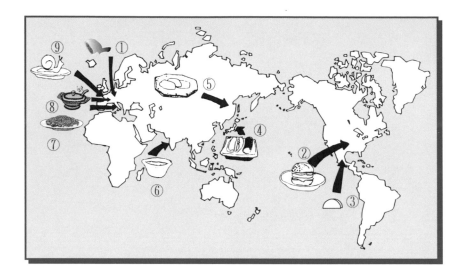

_____ curry   _____ sushi   _____ dim sum

_____ snails   _____ pig knuckle   _____ fondue

_____ hamburger   _____ pasta   _____ taco

CONVERSATION I
Going out for dinner

Brook: Say, do you want to go out for dinner tonight?

Eric: Sure. Where would you like to go?

Brook: What do you think of Thai food?

CHAPTER 6

Eric: I love it, but I'm not really in the mood for it today.

Brook: Yeah. I'm not either, I guess. It's a bit spicy and sour.

Eric: Hmm. How do you like Japanese food?

Brook: Oh, I like it a lot.

Eric: I do, too. And I know a nice Japanese restaurant near here... it's called Fuji.

Brook: Oh, I've always wanted to go there.

Eric: Terrific！ Let's go！

USEFUL EXPRESSIONS

1. Have you tried any exotic food?
   你嚐過任何異國風味的食物嗎？

2. What kind of food would you prefer?
   你喜歡哪類的食物？

3.
   I like | French
Chinese
Italian
Japanese
Mexican
German | food/cuisine.

我喜歡 法國
中國
義大利
日本
墨西哥
德國
菜／料理。

4. A: Have you tried sushi?

   B: No, I haven't, but I'd like to try.

   A: 你吃過壽司嗎?

   B: 沒有,但我想嚐嚐看。

5. A: Have you ever eaten at a Mexican restaurant?

   B: Yes, I have. The food was delicious.

   A: 你去過墨西哥餐廳嗎?

   B: 是的,我曾經去過。那裡的食物美味極了。

CHAPTER 6

LISTENING I

Listen to TV report and check the three most popular kinds of food For each city.

French Thai Italian American Chinese Japanese Mexican German

Tokyo   ∨

London

New York

EXERCISE

1. Write down three of your favorite kinds of food. Then find out what everyone's three favorite kinds of food are in your class.

2. Figure out the top three most popular kinds of food.

CONVERSATION II
In a Japanese restaurant

Waitress: Good evening. Here's our menu. We serve a great variety of popular Japanese dishes in set courses and a la carte. Many guests also like to order the

shabu-shabu.

Brook: What's shabu-shabu?

Waitress: It's a hot pot dish. We put meat, seafood, and
vegetables in it.

Brook: I see.

Eric: What kind of food is the tempura?

Waitress: It's prawns, fish, and assorted vegetables dipped in
batter and then deep fried until crisp. It's a very
popular Japanese food.

Eric: It sounds good. We'll have two prawn and vegetable
tempura.

Waitress: I don't think you want to miss one of the chef's
specialities... globe fish sashimi. It's out of this
world.

Eric: Well, I'll take the raw fish, too. But my wife doesn't
care for it. Could she have something else instead?

Waitress: Certainly, sir. I would recommend you to order the
"chawanmushi" which is the steamed egg custard
with fish cake, mushroom and shrimp.

Brook: O.K. I'll try that.

Waitress: Would you like something to drink with your

CHAPTER 6

meal?

Eric: Yes. I'll have sake and my wife will have green tea, please.

Waitress: Certainly, sir.

USEFUL EXPRESSIONS

1. What kind of dish is the "Nicoise salad"?
   「尼斯沙拉」是什麼？

2. What's this sauce for?
   這個醬料是用來作什麼的？

3. Please put a little of this horseradish sauce in the soy sauce, mix well and then dip the raw fish in it before eating.
   請把芥末醬放在醬油裡，攪拌好，在吃生魚片以前沾一些。

4. This is a dish for two persons.
   這道菜是兩人份的。

5. What time do you open?
   你們幾點開始營業？

6. We open from 11:00 a.m. to 10:00 p.m. ,but our last call for orders is at 9:00 p.m.

餐飲英語

本店從早上十一點開始營業至晚上十點，但九點過後就不接受客人點餐了。

READING

Read the article and write the answers in full sentences.

*　　　*　　　*

The Chinese eat a variety of foods and avoid very few. Rice is the staple food of southern China. Sticky glutinous rice is used occasionally, mainly in sweet dishes. Wheat is the primary staple in the north. It is popular as noodles, dumplings, and pancakes. Thin, square wheat-flour wrappers are used to make fried egg rolls or wontons with a meat, vegetable, or mixed filling which is served either fried or in soup. Most Chinese food is cooked; very little raw food, except fruit, is eaten. Hot soup or tea is the beverage that usually accompanies a meal.

*　　　*　　　*

Soy bean products and a wide variety of fish and shellfish are the primary protein sources in the Japanese diet. Fish and shellfish are often eaten raw. Sugar, soy sauce, and vinegar are a basic seasoning mixture. The Japanese use a large amount of seaweed and algae in their cooking for seasoning, as a wrapping, or in salads and soups. Green tea is the preferred beverage with meals. Sake or beer is often served with dinner. The traditional Japanese diet is low in fat and cholesterol.

Misoshiru is a thick soup made from miso (a paste of fermented soy beans and rice) and dashi (a soup stock made from dried seaweed and bonito fish). Misoshiru is not eaten with a spoon but drunk straight from the bowl.

*   *   *

In the seventeenth century, the method for producing sparkling wine was discovered by the monk Dom Perignon. Today, the champagne bearing his name, Dom Perignon, is considered one of the finest in the world.

France's cuisine is admired and imitated around the world. It implies a carefully planned meal that balances and flavors the dishes. Sauces are the soul of French cooking. They are prepared from stocks that are simmered for hours to bring out the flavor of the ingredients. Always using the freshest, best-tasting ingredients is one of the common rules in preparing French dishes. Wine is an integral part of the meal and must complement the food.

*   *   *

CHAPTER 6

Many people think of Italian cooking as consisting of pizza and spaghetti. In reality, these dishes are only a small part of the regional cuisine of southern Italy. The Italians eat more rice than any other European people. Olive oil is a common ingredient used in almost all cooking. Seasonings common to all of Italy are garlic, parsley, and basil.

Espresso, which means "made expressly for you", is made from finely ground Italian roast coffee through which water is forced by steam pressure. Cappuccino is espresso topped with frothy, steamed milk.

*　　　*　　　*

A lot of people associate the cooking of Mexico with chillis. Although chillis are used frequently, not all Mexican dishes are hot and spicy. Other foods, such as

A "taco" is a fried corn chip stuffed with fillings, such as spicy ground beef, cheese, chopped onion, lettuce, and tomatoes, and served with a spicy sauce on top.

beans, cocoa, corn, and tomatoes add equally important flavors to the cuisine. Mexico is famous for its "stuffed" foods, such as tacos, tortillas and burritos.

＊ ＊ ＊

1. What are the primary protein sources in the Japanese diet?

_____

2. What are the major ingredients Mexican cooking has?

_____

3. What's the staple of north China? How do people use it to make all kinds of dishes?

_____

4. What are the seasonings which are commonly used by Italians?

_____

5. How do the French usually prepare their sauces?

_____

CHAPTER 6

LISTENING II

Listen to this letter written by Pearl to her sister, Brenda. Fill in the right answers.

1. When is Brenda going to Los Angeles?

_____

2. How many different kinds of food does Pearl mention?

_____

3. What does she recommend at the Mexican restaurant?

_____

PAIR WORK

Read the dialog below:

Student A: What food is a specialty of <u>France</u>?

Student B: <u>Escargots</u>.

Student A: What's that?

Student B: It's <u>snails</u>.

Student A: Have you ever tried <u>snails</u>?

Student B: Yes.

Student A: What did they <u>taste</u> like? Did you like them?

Now in pairs, ask and answer similar questions about these other local specialities.

(a) Italy, beef carpaccio (thin sliced raw beef).

(b) Switzerland, fondue (melted chocolate dip).

(c) Mexico, beef fajitas (a kind of corn bread with beef and chopped tomatoes).

(d) France, bouillabaisse (seafood soup).

GRAMMAR FOCUS

1. So, too, neither, either

I like Chinese food a lot.	I don't like greasy food.
So do I. /I do, too.	Neither do I. /I don't either.
Really? I don't like it very much.	Oh, I like it a lot.
I'm crazy about chocolate.	I'm not in the mood for Greek food.
So am I./ I am, too.	Neither am I./ I'm not either.
Oh, I'm not at all.	Really? I am.
I can eat really spicy food.	I can't stand sour food.
So can I./ I can, too.	Neither can I./I can't either.
Oh, I can't.	Oh, I love it.

CHAPTER 6

2. Past tense & Present tense

past tense: events completed
at a definite time in the past.

present perfect: events within
a time period up to the present.

Did you eat goose liver at the restaurant last night? Yes, I did.	Have you ever eaten pheasant? Yes, I have.
Did you go to Canada last summer? No, I didn't.	Have you been to Africa? No, I haven't.
I went to a German restaurant last Sunday.	I have never been to a German restaurant.

Complete these conversations:

(a) A: Have you ever _____ (try) French food?

B: Yes, I _____. It's wonderful.

(b) A: _____ you eat out last night?

B: No, I _____. I cooked at home.

(c) A: _____ you ever _____ (eat) frog's legs?

B: No, I _____.

(d) A: _____ you go to a movie yesterday?

B: Yes, I _____. The movie was good.

VOCABULARY & PHRASES

Nouns

map	seaweed
sushi	protein
dim sum	pasta
fondue	steamed egg custard
tempura	wonton
batter	cholesterol
globe fish	stock
sashimi	soy bean
fish cake	ingredient
sake	bouillabaisse
staple food	pheasant

Adjective

ethnic food	exotic
Thai	be in the mood for ...
Japanese	popular
French	out of this world
Italian	primary
Mexican	traditional

CHAPTER 6

German   bonito fish

errific

<u>Verbs</u>

ferment   imitate

CHAPTER 7

CHAPTER 7

DRINKS

BEVERAGE LIST

- Alcoholic beverages～spirits, liqueurs
- Beer～bottled, draft
- Cocktails～Pink lady, Margarita
- Non-alcoholic/soft drinks～coke, root beer
- Juices～orange, grapefruit
- Mineral water～Volvic, Evian
- Coffee～espresso, Irish
- Tea～orange pekoe, earl grey

WINE LIST

- Champagne～Moet Chandon, Dom Perignon
- White wine～Burgundy white wine
- Red wine～bordeaux red wine
- Rosé～French rosé

Put each of the following drinks in its proper heading below.

For example: Liqueurs: Advocaat

Perrier, sprite, cognac, dubonnet, Mai Tai, ginger ale, dry sherry, Galliano, Evian, vermouth, Long island iced tea, Pina

CHAPTER 7

Colada, lemonade, Scotch whisky, tonic water, rum, Advocaat, Cointreau.

Aperitifs:

Liqueurs:

Cocktails:

Spirits:

Mineral water:

Non-alcoholic/soft drinks:

CONVERSATION I
Recommending an aperitif

Waiter: Good evening. I'm Steven, and I'm your waiter for today. Would you care for something to drink before your meal?

Man: Yes, I think we will. In fact, we have something to celebrate today. It's my wife's birthday.

Waiter: Happy birthday, madam.

Man: I think it calls for something special. What would you recommend?

Waiter: How about a champagne for madam and a sherry for

you, sir?

Man: What would you like, dear?

Woman: Champagne sounds good. I'll try it.

Man: I think I'll have a dubonnet instead of the sherry.

Waiter: Certainly, sir. A champagne for madam and a dubonnet for you. Just a moment, please.

USEFUL EXPRESSIONS

1. Would you like to have something to drink before your meal?

   May I take your drink order first?

   Would you prefer to have a drink first?

   在您用餐前要先來點飲料嗎？

   您要先點飲料嗎？

2. Here's our wine/beverage list.

   這是我們的酒／飲料單。

3.

   I'd like
   | an aperitif. |
   | something non-alcoholic. |
   | a liqueur. |
   | some mineral water. |
   | a cocktail. |

我想要點一杯
> 開胃酒。
> 無酒精飲料。
> 香甜酒。
> 礦泉水。
> 雞尾酒。

4. Would you like to try the dry vermouth?

   您想不想試試看較不甜的苦艾酒？

5. A dry sherry and martini are both very popular with our guests.

   沒甜味的雪利酒及馬丁尼酒都是很受客人喜愛的。

6. 依照飲用時機之不同，酒精性飲料可分為：

   (a) aperitif（開胃酒）

   　　是為了增進食慾，在飯前所飲用的酒。例如：
   vermouth, campari, dubonnet, cocktail等。

   (b) table wine（佐餐酒）

   　　最常見的是red wine, white wine及rosé等。white
   wine及rosé酒性溫和，必須加以冰藏約6℃～8℃下
   飲用。red wine則在常溫18℃～22℃中喝，不需冰
   鎮。

   (c) after dinner drinks（飯後酒）

餐飲英語

用過餐後，通常可選些酒精度較高的酒飲用。例
如：sherry, port, brandy等。

CONVERSATION II

Sommelier: Good evening, sir. Would you like to order
something to drink with your meal?

Guest 1: Yes.

Sommelier: Here's our wine list.

Guest 1: You seem to have a very extensive cellar.

Sommelier: Yes, we've imported a variety of wines from
France, Italy, Germany, U.S.A., Chile, and
Australia.

Guest 1: I see. Well, I like something dry.

Sommelier: The Woodbridge Cabernet Sauvignon possesses
mixture of aromatic and dry in taste.

Guest 1: Alright. I'll have a glass of it.

Guest 2: What kind of wine would be suitable for my pan
fried Dover sole?

Sommelier: I would recommend our house wine, dry

Bordeaux white wine. It would go very well with your Dover sole. It's a Bordeaux with a rich but delicate body.

Guest 2: That sounds good. I'll have it.

Sommelier: I'll be right back with your drinks.

Guest 2: Thank you.

USEFUL EXPRESSIONS

1. 品嚐wine時，注意其：

   (a) color（顏色）

   (b) smell = aroma = bouquet（香味）

   (c) taste（味道）

   酒在口中時，留意下列四項要：

   (a) body（濃郁度）：light, medium, full-bodied

   (b) acidity（果酸度）：自然果酸的酸味

   (c) tannin（單寧酸）：石碳酸的澀味

   (d) sweetness（甜味）：酒中剩餘糖分，可區分為sweet, medium sweet

   另有不甜的酒，其口感可區分為dry, medium dry

2. 其他形容酒的用詞有：sparkling（帶有氣泡的）, fruity（帶有果香的）。

3. The rosé wine would go very well with your pan fried Norwegain salmon.

   這種粉紅酒十分適合搭配您的香煎挪威鮭魚。

4. This champagne, clear in color with layers of aromatic taste, fits well with all kinds of food.

   這香檳酒味細膩豐富，具多層次水果芳香，適合搭配各類食物。

5. This white wine from California tastes rich and full-bodied and is a great match with roasted and grilled meat and a variety of pasta.

   這款來自加州的白酒，口感渾厚圓潤，適合搭配煎烤類或義大利麵食等食物。

6. This classical white wine from Italy, with a slightly acidic palate, accompanies white meat and seafood entrees very well.

   這款義大利白酒，口感略帶酸澀，可搭配雞肉或海鮮。

7. This red wine, well balanced, elegant in taste, with a good structure Of tannin, goes very well with cold cuts, lightly flavored duck, and beef dishes.

   這款紅酒，口感細緻平衡，前味優雅，適合搭配前菜沙拉或牛肉。

8.

I'll have  of red wine.

我想要  紅酒。

9. What do you suggest as a table wine?

你推薦什麼樣的佐餐酒？

10. 形容飲料不同類型的講法：

an alcoholic drink ↔ an soft/non-alcoholic drink

a dry sherry ↔ a sweet sherry

light beer ↔ strong beer

a single whisky ↔ a double whisky

draft beer ↔ bottled/canned beer

still mineral water ↔ sparkling/carbonated mineral water

CONVERSATION III

Heather: Hey, this place looks cool.

Timmy: I told you it was a good pub. Where do you want to

sit?

Heather: Well ... let's sit at the bar.

Bartender: What can I get for you two?

Heather: I'm not quite sure. Can you recommend a couple of cocktails for me?

Bartender: Well, what do you usually like to drink?

Heather: I prefer something with fruity flavor.

Bartender: How about a Blue Hawaii for you?

Heather: What's that?

Bartender: It's a drink made with Bacardi rum, Curacao blue,pineapple juice, and coconut milk. It's a very popular tropical style cocktail.

Heather: O.K., I'll have it.

Bartender: And for you, sir?

Jimmy: I think I'll have something sharp tonight. Make me a double Scotch with no ice, please. Oh, by the way, when will the band start?

Bartender: It starts at 9:30.

CHAPTER 7

USEFUL EXPRESSIONS

1. Guest:

I'd like	
I think I'll have	a gin.
Can you get me	

Server:

How do you like your gin?
On the rocks, straight up or with tonic water/soda?

客人：我想要一杯琴酒。

調酒員：是要加冰塊、純喝或加通寧水？

2. Please give me a single whisky with ice.

Please give me a single whisky on the rocks.

請給我一杯單份加冰塊的威士忌。

3. Would you care for another drink?

How about another drink?

Can I fix you another drink?

您還想要再來一杯嗎？

4. We have imported and domestic beer.

我們有進口及國產的啤酒。

5. This champagne isn't chilled enough.

   這香檳不夠冰。

6. 調製cocktail時，常使用的garnish有：

   orange slice（柑橘片），lemon slice（檸檬片），pineapple slice（鳳梨切片），cherry（櫻桃），olive（橄欖），salt（鹽），pearl onion（珍珠洋蔥），celery stalk（芹菜桿），lime wedge（楔形青檸檬），lime wheel（青檸檬圈）。

7. 調製cocktail，所使用的器材有：

   shaker（搖酒器），mixing glass（攪拌杯），strainer（濾酒器），bar spoon（調酒匙），measure/jigger（量酒器），ice bucket（冰桶），ice tong（冰夾），corkscrew（螺旋式開瓶器），stirrer（調酒棒），squeezer（擠壓器），bottle/can opener（開瓶器／開罐器），blender（果汁機），pourer（倒酒器），cutting board（切板），cocktail stick（雞尾酒籤），coaster（杯墊），straw（吸管）。

CHAPTER 7

CONVERSATION IV

Waiter: Good afternoon. What would you like to drink, please?

Peter: What do you want, Emily?

Emily: Well, I'd like to have the herbal tea.

Waiter: And what about you, sir?

Peter: I'll have a cup of coffee.

Waiter: All right. We have excellent Colombian, Blue Mountain, Brazilian, espresso, cappuccino, Coffee Latte, Irish coffee, and decaffeinated.

Peter: I'll go for the Colombian, please.

Waiter: OK. Would you like something to eat as well?

Emily: I'll have fruit tart.

Peter: Can you get me some cream puffs, please?

Waiter: Certainly.

*   *   *

Emily: How do you like your coffee?

Peter: It's great ... aromatic, smooth, rich and gives a delicate

flavor. That's just what I like.

Emily: That's good. I love the smell of coffee and all kinds of desserts with coffee flavor. But I just don't drink it often. It always keeps me awake.

Peter: Oh, what a pity. I usually have a cup of coffee at my breakfast. It refreshes me. Maybe next time you can try decaffeinated coffee. It contains a lot less caffeine than regular coffee and tastes good as well.

USEFUL EXPRESSIONS

1. decaffeinated coffee指的是low in caffeine的咖啡。在一般餐廳中，喝咖啡所加的糖，可選擇的有：white sugar（白糖），brown sugar（黑糖）或artificial sweetener（代糖）。至於奶精方面則有：milk（牛奶），cream（奶精）可選擇。

2. 所謂的單品咖啡，較著名的有：
Colombian（哥倫比亞），Brazilian（巴西），Blue Mountain（藍山），Mandeling（曼特寧），Mocha（摩卡），Java（爪哇），Kenya（肯亞），Cona（科那）。

3. Basic coffee making

Type	Description	Ingredients	Preparation
Espresso	Strong & short	· espresso coffee	The espresso always has to be strong & short.
Cappuccino	Espresso with foamed milk.	· espresso coffee · foameded milk · cinnamon powder/cocoa powder	· Make an espresso · Fill with Foamed milk . · Add cinnamon powder on the top.
Coffee Latte	Espresso with steamed milk	· ⅓ espresso coffee · ⅔ steamed milk	· Make an espresso. · Pour steamed milk up to the top.
Irish coffee	Freshly brewed coffee with Irish whisky.	· coffee · sugar · 1 oz Irish whisky · whipped cream	· Heat the glass and melt the sugar. · Burn Irish Whisky in the glass. · Pour coffee into the glass. · Fill up with whipped cream.

與coffee有關的字彙：

instant coffee　　　　　即溶咖啡

instant coffee pack　　　即溶咖啡隨身包

foamed milk	奶泡
whipped cream	打發的鮮奶油
cinnamon powder	肉桂粉
cocoa powder	可可粉
steamed milk	熱牛奶

LISTENING

You will hear three customers ordering several drinks each. Write down all the names of the drinks they order and the information they give to the barman.

Customer 1: _____

Customer 2: _____

Customer 3: _____

VOCABULARY & PHRASES

<u>Nouns</u>

beverage list	decaffeinated coffee
alcoholic beverage	caffeine
spirit	artificial sweetener
liqueurs	cocktail
(bottled/draft) beer	cellar

non-alcoholic/soft drinks

root beer

mineral water

orange pekoe

wine list

champagne

aroma

tannin

mixture

sommelier

herbal tea

Adjectives

sparkling

a variety of ...

imported

domestic

straight up = without ice

on the rocks = with ice

garnish

(orange) slice

straw

coaster

shaker

herbal tea

instant coffee

steamed milk

foamed milk

still

extensive

tropical

CHAPTER 8

CHAPTER 8

FAST FOOD RESTAURANT

MATCHING

_____ 1. I'd like two cups of _____.   a. go

_____ 2. Please give me a large order of _____. b. cole slaw

_____ 3. Is that for here or to _____ ?   c. chicken

_____ 4. I'd like a turkey _____.   d. iced tea

_____ 5. I'd like nine pieces of _____.   e. soda

_____ 6. Please give me a container of _____.   f. milk shake

_____ 7. I'd like a small orange _____.   g. French fries

_____ 8. I'd like a strawberry _____.   h. sandwich

CONVERSATION I
At a fast food restaurant

Debby: I'm hungry.

Tiffany: Me, too. Let's go to a restaurant.

Debby: O.K., but I'm in a hurry. We can't take too much time.

Tiffany: All right. Let's find a fast food restaurant.

Debby: Okay.

Tiffany: Oh！Look, Debby, here's one.

CHAPTER 8

Debby: How's the food?

Tiffany: It's pretty good.

Debby: Should we eat here or should we take our food with us?

Tiffany: Let's get it to go. You're in a hurry. It'll save time.

Debby: Okay.

*   *   *

Debby: What are you gonna order?

Tiffany: I don't know. Let's look at the menu.

Debby: Look, they have hamburgers here and chicken nuggets.

Tiffany: I think I'll get chicken nuggets.

Debby: I'm gonna get a hamburger and onion rings.

Tiffany: There aren't many people here but we'll still have to stand in line.

Debby: Where should we stand in line?

Tiffany: This one is shorter. Let's stand here.

Cashier: Welcome to Burger Queen. May I help you?

Debby: Yes, I'll have a hamburger and onion rings.

Tiffany: I'd like six pieces of chicken nuggets and a small order of French fries.

Cashier: Would you like anything to drink?

Debby: An iced lemon tea, please.

Tiffany: And I'll have Sprite.

Cashier: Actually, you might want to order our "Value meal" instead of ordering the items separately. It'll save you some money.

Debby: All right, then. We'll have the value meals.

Cashier: Is that for here or to go?

Tiffany: To go, please.

Cashier: All right. Coming right up!

            *   *   *

Cashier: Here you are, ma'am. And that comes to two hundred and thirty dollars.

Tiffany: There you go.

Cashier: Thank you very much.

USEFUL EXPRESSIONS

1. Menu of a fast food restaurant:

Hamburger	漢堡
Sandwich	三明治
Fried chicken	炸雞

CHAPTER 8

Pizza	比薩
Taco	墨西哥脆餅
Spaghetti	義大利麵
<u>Side Orders</u>	<u>附餐類</u>
French fries (large/medium/small)	薯條（大／中／小）
Hot crispy pie (apple/pineapple)	派（蘋果／鳳梨）
Baked potato	烤馬鈴薯
Onion rings	洋蔥圈
Cole slaw	涼拌包心菜
Sundae	聖代
Ice cream cone	冰淇淋
Hot soup	熱湯
Milk shake	奶昔
Biscuit	比司吉
<u>Beverages</u>	<u>飲料類</u>
Coke/Pepsi	可樂
Diet coke	健怡可樂
Sprite/Fanta	雪碧／芬達
Iced lemon tea	冰檸檬紅茶
Orange juice	柳橙汁
Hot coffee	熱咖啡

Hot tea	熱紅茶
Hot chocolate	熱巧克力
Lemonade	檸檬汁

2. deli（delicatessen）是專賣三明治，沙拉之類熟食的店。如果客人點了一種sandwich，則counter helper會問你 "Will that be on white, rye, whole wheat bread, or croissant?" 是問你要哪種麵包。客人可回答 "On whole wheat (or rye/white/croissant), please."

3. "What would you like with your sandwich?"
是問你三明治要加什麼配料。通常可選擇的有：sliced tomato, lettuce, pickle, onion, ketchup, mustard, mayonnaise, cheese等配料。

4. 在速食店裡點fried chicken常見的部位有：drumstick（雞腿）, breast（雞胸）, wing（翅）。炸雞的計算單位用piece。例如：two pieces of chicken wings。

5. 在fast food restaurant時，placing an order的說法：

a container of cole slaw	一盒涼拌包心菜
a cup of coffee	一杯咖啡
a piece of fried chicken	一塊炸雞
a mall/large order of French fries	一包小／大薯條
a large/medium/small coke	一杯大／中／小可樂

CHAPTER 8

| two cups of coffee | 兩杯咖啡 |
| two pieces of fried chicken | 兩塊炸雞 |

CONVERSATION II
Ordering a pizza by phone

Waiter: Pizza House. May I help you?

Jason: Yes, I'd like to order a pizza.

Waiter: What toppings would you like on your pizza?

Jason: I'd like to order a style pizza. What kind of styles do you have?

Waiter: If you are a seafood lover, we have Seafood pizza with shrimps, crabs, squids, clams, and peas on it. And if you like something spicy, our Mexican pizza with onion, Jalapeno peppers, and sausage would be an excellent choice. The Veggie is suitable for vegetarians. The Super supreme contains the most toppings of all.

Jason: I think I'll have one nine-inch Super supreme with deep dish crust and two pieces of garlic bread.

Waiter: All right. Pick up or delivery?

Jason: Could you please deliver it to the following address?

Waiter Okay. We'll deliver it in fifteen minutes.

USEFUL EXPRESSIONS

1. 一般會加在pizza上的配料（topping）：

ham（火腿）	beef（牛肉）
sausage（美式香腸）	pepperoni（義式肉腸）
anchovies（鯷魚）	shrimp（蝦子）
squid（墨魚）	onion（洋蔥）
olive（黑橄欖）	green pepper（青椒）
pineapple（鳳梨）	mushroom（蘑菇）
pea（青豆）	corn（玉米）
clam（蛤蜊肉）	

   至於pizza皮（crust）方面，亦可選擇：

   薄片：thin

   厚片：thick or deep dish

2. order pizza時，店員會問：

   "For here, pick up or delivery?"

   指在店內用餐，外帶或外送。

3. pizza的size 可分為標準9 inches的或13 inches的。另外
   也可以點單片的，其單位以 "slice" 來形容。例如：

CHAPTER 8

I'd like two slices of Hawaiian pizza.

LISTENING

A family is ordering food at Corner Cafe. Listen and check the items you hear.

Mother: _____

Daughter: _____

Son: _____

Father: _____

Look at this conversation at a fast food restaurant. Decide where the sentences a-g go in the conversation.

Cashier: Good afternoon. May I help you?

Customer: (1) _____.

Cashier: Would you like a regular or a large soda?

Customer: (2) _____.

Cashier: Would you like anything else?

Customer: (3) _____.

Cashier: What flavor would you like?

餐飲英語

Customer: (4) _____.

Cashier: O.K.

Customer: (5) _____.

Cashier: That's one hundred twenty six dollars, please.

Customer: (6) _____.

Cashier: Thank you.

a. Regular

b. Good afternoon. Yes, I'd like a grilled cheeseburger with onion rings and an orange soda.

c. Strawberry, please.

d. How much is that?

e. Yes, I'd like some ice cream, please.

f. Here you are.

ACTIVITY

A: Welcome to Deli Express. May I help you?

B: Yes. I'd like a roast beef sandwich and a baked potato.

A: Would you like anything to drink?

B: Yes. I'll have a small Pepsi.

A: Okay. That's a roast beef sandwich, a baked potato, and a small Pepsi. Is that for here or to go?

B: For here.

A: That comes to one hundred and forty dollars, please.

B: Here you are.

A: And here's your change. Your food will be ready in a moment.

B: Thank you.

Use the above conversation as an example to practice ordering food at a fast food restaurant.

1.

a cheeseburger

a large order of French fries

BURGER QUEEN

a strawberry milk shake

to go

$ 105

2.

a tuna fish sandwich

a small salad

a hot soup

DELI EXPRESS

for here

$ 140

3.

13-inch pizza

two apple pies

five medium coke

PIZZA HOUSE

for here

$ 465

4.

18 pieces of fried chicken

2 containers of cole slaw

2 lemonades

Fried Chicken Factory

to go

$ 375

5.

2 tacos

2 bowls of chili

2 orange soda

Taco Bell

to go

$ 180

PAIR WORK

Talk with a partner about fast food restaurants.

— Are there fast food restaurants in your city or town?

— What do they serve?

— Do you ever go to fast food restaurants?

— If so, where do you go?

— What do you usually order?

— Do you like the food?

— Is that food good for you?

— Why do many people go to fast food restaurants?

As a class, discuss students "fast-food" experience.

VOCABULARY & PHRASES

Nouns

milk shake	pickle
chicken nugget	chicken drumstick
onion ring	style pizza
sundae	pepperoni
biscuit	anchovy

lemonade	delivery
croissant	crust
whole wheat bread	crab

<u>Verb</u>

to stand in line

CHAPTER 9

CHAPTER 9

TALKING ABOUT MONEY

CONVERSATION

Customer: Could I have my bill, please?

Waiter: Certainly, sir. One moment, please. Here's your check, sir.

Customer: Thank you. What's this item here? Number 2.

Waiter: That's the cover charge, sir.

Customer: OK. I don't understand this: you seem to have charged me twice for the drink. Look at items 6 and 8.

Waiter: I'll just go and check it for you, sir. Yes, sir, you're right. the cashier made a mistake. We're very sorry about this. I think you'll find it's correct now.

Customer: Oh, that's all right. Thank you. Does the bill include service charge?

Waiter: The bill doesn't include service charge, sir. If you would like to give the server tip, that's at your discretion.

Customer: I see.

CHAPTER 9

Waiter: How would you like to pay, sir? Cash, or charge?

Customer: I'll pay in cash. Here it is.

Waiter: Do you need to put company invoice number on the receipt?

Customer: No, thank you.

Waiter: Thank you. I'll be right back with your change and receipt.

*   *   *

Waiter: Here's your change and receipt.

Customer: Oh, keep the change.

Waiter: Thank you very much, sir. It's a pleasure serving you. Hope to see you again soon.

USEFUL EXPRESSIONS

1. I'd like to settle my bill?
   我想買單。

2. Your bill comes to five thousand nine hundred and twenty-six NT dollars.
   您的帳單總共是新台幣五千九百二十六元。

3. A 8% tax and a 10% service charge has been added to your bill.

Your bill includes a 8% tax and a 10% service charge.

百分之八的稅和百分之十的服務費已經加在您的帳單裡了。

4. You don't have to pay any extra for tax, sir. It's already in the price of the meal.

您不需再額外付稅，它已內含在餐點的價錢中了。

5. The restaurant will be closing in half an hour. May I close your bill now?

本餐廳再過半小時就要打烊了，我現在能先為您結帳嗎？

6. Would you like a separate check?

您們的帳單要分開算嗎？

7. I'd like to sign to my room.

我想簽房帳。

8. How will you be paying?

How would you like to pay?

請問您要以什麼方式付帳？

9. I'll pay in

cash.
US dollars/Japanese yen/etc.

I'll pay by

credit card.
traveller's check.
personal check.

我付

現金。
美元。
日幣。

我用

信用卡
旅行支票
個人支票

來付帳。

10. That'll be fine, sir/madam.
    沒問題。

11.

I'm sorry, sir/madam. We don't

accept ... credit card.
honor traveller's checks.
accept foreign currency as payment.
accept personal checks.

很抱歉，我們這裡不接受用 | ……信用卡
 旅行支票
 外幣
 私人支票 | 付帳。

12. I'll ask the manager/cashier about that.

    我去詢問一下經理／櫃枱出納。

13. By which card will you be paying?

    In which currency would you like to pay?

    您要用哪種信用卡付帳？

    您要哪國的貨幣付帳？

14. Could you please sign your name here?

    麻煩您在這裡簽名。（使用簽帳卡的情況下）

15. Could you please make out your check to Red Lobster?

    請您在支票的抬頭上寫「紅龍蝦餐廳」。

16. May I have your company invoice number?

    請問您公司的統一編號是幾號？

17. Customer: Do you take credit card?

    Waiter: Yes, we accept most credit cards.

    顧客：你們接受信用卡付帳嗎？

    服務人員：是的，我們接受大部分的信用卡。

18. How much do you add for service?

    你們服務費加了多少？

19. 到餐廳用餐時，有的客人會視情形給予服務人員tip
    （小費）。但如果是到cafeterias或fast food restaurants
    則不需另給服務生小費。

20. farewell to the guests:

    Have a nice afternoon/evening/weekend, sir/madam.

    Good night (Good bye), sir/madam. Hope to see you
    again soon.

    Thank you for coming.

    I hope you enjoy your meal.

    We look forward to serving you again.

    It's a pleasure to serve you.

    客人要離開時：

    祝您有個愉快的下午／夜晚／週末。

    晚安（再見），希望您早日再度光臨。

    謝謝光臨。

    希望您用餐滿意。

    期待再度為您服務。

    能為您服務是我們的榮幸。

LISTENING

1. You will hear six customers asking about paying their bills. Add any details in the last column.

2. Then listen again. Listen carefully to what the waiter/waitress reply to their customers. Put a tick (∨) on the column if the restaurant can accept the payment the customer ask for. Put a (×) on the column if the restaurant cannot accept the customers' payment.

	Cash	Foreign Currency	Traveller's check	Credit card	Personal check	Details
1				∨		American Express card
2						
3						
4						
5						
6						

CHAPTER 9

PAIR WORK

Work with a partner. Make up some bills. Take turns to be W (a waiter/waitress) and C (a customer). Practice the conversation as the following situations:

(a) starts from the moment when customer asks for the bill until he or she gets the receipt.

(b) the cashier didn't correctly add up the check.

VOCABULARY & PHRASES

Nouns

bill/check	Japanese yen
credit card	foreign currency
traveller's check	cover charge
company invoice number	personal check
receipt	cashier
change	tip
service charge	extra
US dollar	NT dollar

Verbs

sign	charge

餐飲英語

<u>Adjective</u>

be at someone's discretion

CHAPTER 10

CHAPTER 10

BREAKFAST

餐飲英語

1. Match the food items in the pictures with the words in the list.

(a)_____

(b) _____

(c)_____

(d) _____

CHAPTER 10

_____ green tea	_____ milk
_____ tomato & mushroom	_____ salted egg
_____ fish	_____ pickled cucumber
_____ miso soup	_____ coffee
_____ seaweed	_____ rice
_____ toast	_____ dried pork
_____ orange juice	_____ beancurd
_____ congee	_____ gluten
_____ ham	_____ tea
_____ sausage	_____ pickled plum
_____ eggs	

2. Listen and check your answers.

3. Listen to the conversations and label the pictures as Chinese breakfast, American breakfast, England breakfast and Japanese breakfast.

CONVERSATION I

A: What do you usually have for breakfast?

B: Cereal with milk and fresh fruit.

A: Sounds healthy.

B: Yeah. What about you?

A: I have coffee and toast. But if I'm in a rush, I skip my breakfast.

B: Having breakfast is very important for your health. It gives you a lot of energy. By the way, have you had breakfast yet?

A: Not yet.

B: Me, neither. Let's have breakfast at a fast food restaurant together. I want to have the hash brown there.

B: Okay.

PAIR WORK

Ask and answer the following questions with a partner. Then add three questions of your own.

(a) Do you usually have breakfast in the morning?

(b) What do you usually eat?

(c) Do you ever eat meat or fish for breakfast?

(d) Do you ever go to a restaurant for breakfast?

(e) Do you always drink the same thing for breakfast?

(f) Name one thing you never have for breakfast.

(g) What do people eat for breakfast in your country and other countries you've been to?

GRAMMAR FOCUS

I
| always |
| usually |
| often |
| sometimes |
| seldom |
| never |
have breakfast.

100%	always
	usually
	often
	sometimes
	seldom
0%	never

Add the adverbs to the sentences. Then practice the conversation with a partner.

餐飲英語

A: What do you have for breakfast? (usually)

B: Well, I have sausage, pancake, and coffee on Sundays. (often)

A: Do you eat breakfast at work? (ever)

B: Yes, I have breakfast at my desk. (sometimes)

A: Do you eat cereal for breakfast? (ever)

B: I don't have cereal. (often)

EXERCISE

Number the following statements in the correct order to make a conversation. Then practice the conversation.

___ Yes, please.   ___ How many eggs do you want?

___ Two slices.   ___ What would you like?

___ Do you want toast?___ The bacon and egg special, please.

___ Two, please.   _1_ Are you ready to order?

___ Yes, I am.   ___ How many slices of toast would you like?

CONVERSATION II
Having breakfast at a restaurant

Hubert Lee is at the Hilton in Chicago.

CHAPTER 10

Waitress: Hi！ How are you doing? Are you ready to order?

Hubert: Yes, I'm, thank you. I'll have the American breakfast.

Waitress: An American breakfast. Certainly, sir. What kind of juice would you prefer, carrot, grapefruit, pineapple juice or fruit platter?

Hubert: Freshly squeezed grapefruit juice, please.

Waitress: How would you like your eggs done? Sunny side up, over easy, or ....

Hubert: Sunny side up?

Waitress: Well, that's when the egg's not flipped over. You can also have your eggs poached or scrambled.

Hubert: Uh, I think I'll have them sunny side up.

Waitress: And will that be served with sausage, ham, or bacon?

Hubert: Bacon and make it very crispy, please.

Waitress: You may choose one of the items from our bakery.

Hubert: Danish pastry, please. Could I have the yogurt?

Waitress: Sorry, sir. I'm afraid the yogurt will be a side order.

Hubert: All right, then. A side order of yogurt.

Waitress: And tea or coffee?

Hubert: Coffee, please.

Waitress: Now or later?

Hubert: Now, please.

Waitress: Cream and sugar are on the table. I'll bring your
coffee right away.

Hubert: Thank you.

FIGURE IT OUT

(a) In which way can Hubert Lee have his eggs cooked?

(b) What does sunny side up mean?

(c) What's a side order?

(d) What did Hubert Lee ask for as a side order?

(e) What're included in an American breakfast?

USEFUL EXPRESSIONS

1. 西式早餐一般可分為兩種，一是美式早餐（American
breakfast）；另一種則是歐陸式早餐（Continental
breakfastt）。美式早餐內容相當豐富，包括下列五大
項目：

(a) Juice & Fruit　果汁＆水果

果汁可分成一般的果汁（fruit juice），及新鮮現榨

的果汁（fresh squeezed juice）。常見的果汁及水果
有：

— carrot juice（紅蘿蔔汁）

— watermelon juice（西瓜汁）

— tomato juice（番茄汁）

— orange juice（柳橙汁）

— fruit salad（水果沙拉）

— grapefruit juice（葡萄柚汁）

— pineapple juice（鳳梨汁）

— guava juice（番石榴汁）

— apple juice（蘋果汁）

— seasonal fruit platter（季節鮮果盤）

另外還有燉水果乾：stewed prunes（蜜汁黑棗
乾）、 stewed figs（蜜汁無花果乾）、 stewed
apricots（蜜汁杏乾）。

(b) From the bakery　各類烘培麵包、土司

— bagel（猶太培果）

— croissant（牛角可頌）

— multigrain（雜糧麵包）

— rye bread（全麥麵包）

— Danish pastries（丹麥麵包）

— banana bread（香蕉麵包）

— rolls or toast（小圓麵包或土司）

以上麵包 serve 時，皆會附上 butter（奶油）、marmalade or jam（果醬）。

另外還有：doughnuts（甜甜圈）、French toast（法國土司）、waffle（華富餅）、pancake（煎餅）、muffin（鬆餅）。 waffle, pancake, French toast 在食用時，通常會淋上 jam, maple syrup（楓糖漿）或 honey（蜂蜜）。

(c) Eggs　蛋類

蛋隨著烹煮方法之不同，可以分為：

— Fried eggs（煎蛋）：只煎一面的荷包蛋稱為 sunny side up，兩面煎半熟的則為 over easy。

— Boiled eggs（帶殼水煮蛋）：煮三分鐘熟的叫 soft boiled，煮五分鐘熟的稱之為 hard boiled。

— Poached eggs（去殼水煮蛋）

— Scrambled eggs（炒蛋）

通常任何型態的蛋類，皆可任選搭配 ham（火腿）、sausage（美式香腸）或 bacon（培根）。

— Omelet（蛋捲）：可由客人選擇內含 ham, sausage, bacon, cheddar cheese, diced potatoes,

CHAPTER 10

fresh mushroom, broccoli, tomatoes, onions.

(d) Cereal　穀類食品

指玉米、燕麥等製成的穀類製品，如：

— corn flakes（香酥玉米片）

— honey smacks（蜂蜜裸麥）

— frosted flakes（甜玉米）

— rice crispies（脆爆米）

— bran（裸麥片）

— raisin bran（葡萄乾麥片）

— all bran（全麥片）

— homemade grain and nut cereal（堅果麥片）

食用時通常加上 cold or hot milk（冰或熱牛奶），有時再加上切片的 sliced banana or strawberry（香蕉或草莓）。此外，穀類相關製品還有： oatmeal（燕麥粥）、 cornmeal（玉米粥）。

(e) Beverages　飲料

指 coffee 或 tea 及 chocolate，等不含酒精的飲料。Coffee 可選擇的有 regular coffee（一般咖啡），或 decaffeinated（低咖啡因咖啡）。一般而言，點 coffee 時，有附上 sugar or cream；點 tea 時，則有附上 milk or lemon。

歐陸式早餐比美式早餐簡單，內容大致相同，但
不供應蛋及肉類。客人想點這兩類食品時，得另
外付費。

2. 點餐時，如果 guest 說："I'd like some tea, please."

則 server 應該問："Would you like it with milk or lemon?"

客人：我想點茶。

服務人員：請問您要加牛奶或檸檬？

example I:

Guest: "Can I have some fruit juice, please?"

Server: "Would you like orange juice, grapefruit juice, or watermelon juice?"

範例 I：

客人：我想點果汁。

服務人員：請問您要點柳橙汁、葡萄柚汁或西瓜汁？

example II:

Guest: "I'd like eggs, please."

Server: "Would you like it fried, poached, boiled, or scrambled?"

範例 II：

客人：我想點蛋。

服務人員：請問您是要煎蛋、水煮蛋或炒蛋？

example III:

Guest: "I'd like hot drink, please."

Server: "Would you like coffee, tea, or hot chocolate?"

範例Ⅲ：

客人：我想要熱飲料。

服務人員：請問您是要咖啡、茶或熱巧克力？

example IV:

Guest: "Can I have some coffee, please?"

Server: "Would you like it with cream or sugar?"

範例Ⅳ：

客人：我想點咖啡。

服務人員：請問您是要加奶精或糖？

example V:

Guest: "I'll have scrambled eggs, please."

Server: "What would you like your eggs served with? Ham,
        sausage, or bacon?"

範例Ⅴ：

客人：我想點炒蛋。

服務人員：請問您的蛋要附什麼？火腿、香腸或培
        根？

example VI:

Guest: "I'll have boiled eggs."

Server: "How many minutes shall we boil your eggs?

"Would you like hard-boiled or soft-boiled eggs?"

範例VI：

客人：我想要水煮蛋。

服務人員：您想要煮幾分鐘？

EXERCISE

Fill in the blank column with proper sentences.

Server: Good morning! _____.

Guest: Yes, I am. I'll have tomato juice, please.

Server: _____

Guest: I don't think I want any cereal. I'll have the waffles.

Server: _____

Guest: Honey, please. Then I'll have boiled eggs.

Server: _____

Guest: Five minutes, please.

Server: _____

Guest: Oh, nothing thanks. I'll have them on their own.

Server: _____

Guest: I think I'd like hot chocolate. Thank you very much.

LISTENING

RED ROOF
BREAKFAST MENU
Served from 6:00 am to 11:00 am

AMERICAN BREAKFAST

A Choice of Fruit Juices or Fresh Fruit

Pineapple, Orange, Apple, Carrot, Tomato, Grapefruit, or Watermelon

Mixed Fresh Fruit Platter

Fruit Salad

A Selection of Bakery Basket

Bagel, Croissant, Danish Pastries, Muffin, Banana Bread,

Multigrain, Toast Bread, Rolls, Doughnuts

Served with Jam, Butter, and Marmalade

Buttermilk Pancakes, Pecan Nut Waffles

Served with Honey, Maple syrup, Butter

Two Fresh Eggs
Any Style (Boiled, Scrambled, Poached, Fried)

With your Choice of Bacon, Ham, or Sausage

Fluffy Omelet

With your Choice of Ham, Cheese, Mushrooms, Tomatoes or Onions

Choice of Beverages

Coffee, Decaffeinated Coffee, Tea

With Milk, Cream, Sugar, Lemon

Hot Chocolate

With Hot or Cold Milk

CONTINENTAL BREAKFAST

A Choice of Fresh Juice or Fruit

Watermelon, Apple, Carrot, Grapefruit, Tomato, Pineapple

Fruit platter, Fruit Salad

A Selection of Cereals

Raisin Bran, Corn Flakes, Frosted Flakes, All Bran, Rice Crispy

Your Bakery Basket Filled With

Croissants, Muffins, Danish Pastries, Doughnuts,

Rolls, Toast, Banana Bread

Served with Preserves and Butter

CHAPTER 10

Choice of Beverages

Coffee, Decaffeinated Coffee, Tea

With Milk, Cream, Lemon

TAIWANESE BREAKFAST

Sweeet Potato Congee with Pickled Cucumber, Gluten,

Dried Pork Floss, Beancurd, Pan-fried Eggs with Preserved Radish,

And Chinese Tea

JAPANESE BREAKFAST

Rice, Grilled fish, Marinated Turnip,

Japanese Pickles, Tofu, Miso Soup,

Seasonal fruits, and Japanese Tea

HEALTHY BREAKFAST

Choice of Fruit Juice or Fruit Salad

Choice of All Bran with Skimmed Milk and

Two Low Cholesterol Eggs,

Basket of Multigrain, and Bran-Muffin

with Low Fat Butter, Low-Sugar Jam,

Fruit or Plain Yogurt

Coffee or Tea

餐飲英語

Read through the above menu. Listen to some guests ordering breakfast. Then put a tick (∨) against the right answers.

1. The guest wants

    (a) American breakfast.

    (b) Healthy breakfast.

    (c) Japanese breakfast.

2. The guest wants

    (a) grapefruit juice and all bran.

    (b) orange juice and frosted flakes

    (c) orange juice and corn flakes

3. The guest wants

    (a) fried eggs.

    (b) boiled eggs, cooked for three minutes.

    (c) boiled eggs, cooked for five minutes.

4. The guest wants

    (a) a doughnut and chocolate milk

    (b) a bagel and decaffeinated coffee.

    (c) a croissant and coffee.

5. The guest wants

    (a) omelet with tomatoes, mushrooms and cheese.

(b) omelet with onions, mushrooms, and cheese.

(c) Omelet with tomatoes, cheese and onions.

6. The guest wants

(a) fruit salad, yogurt, and coffee.

(b) grapefruit juice, multigrain, and decaffeinated coffee.

(c) fruit salad, multigrain, and decaffeinated coffee.

PAIR WORK

Use he Red Roof breakfast menu. In pairs, take turns to be customers or waiter/waitress; give and take orders.

VOCABULARY & PHRASES

Nouns

gluten	plain yogurt
pickled cucumber	oatmeal
dried pork	fig
beancurd	guava
congee	bagel
salted	multigrain
seaweed	marmalade
miso soup	Danish pastries

hash brown	doughnut
American/Continental breakfast	French toast
grapefruit	waffle
cereal	pancake
toast	muffin
(fried/boiled/poached/scrambled) eggs	maple syrup
preserve	

CHAPTER 11

CHAPTER 11

ROOM SERVICE

PLEASE HANG ROOM SERVICE
BREAKFAST ORDER OUTSIDE
DOORKNOB BEFORE 2:00 A.M.

Indicate number of breakfast, time required and check each Item required.

No. of breakfasts required ☐ Room no ☐ Date:_____

Preferred service time:

☐ 6:00 ~ 6:30 ☐ 7:30 ~ 8:00 ☐ 9:00 ~ 9:30
☐ 6:30 ~ 7:00 ☐ 8:00 ~ 8:30 ☐ 9:30 ~ 10:00
☐ 7:00 ~ 7:30 ☐ 8:30 ~ 9:00 ☐ 10:00 ~ 10:30

TAIWANESE BREAKFAST 390
Taiwanese Congee
With Pickles, Gluten, Dried Pork, Beancurd, and Salted Egg.
☐ Oolong Tea ☐ Jasmine Tea

CONTINENTAL BREAKFAST 390
Juice:	☐ Orange	☐ Grapefruit	☐ Tomato
	☐ Watermelon	☐ Pineapple	☐ Carrot
Bread:	☐ Muffins	☐ Wholewheat Rolls	☐ Bagel
	☐ Croissants	☐ Danish Pastries	

Served with Jam, Butter, & Marmalade

Yogurt:	☐ Plain	☐ Blueberry ☐ Fruit Flavored	☐ Low Fat
Beverage:	☐ Coffee ☐ Tea		
	With ☐ Cream	☐ Sugar ☐ Milk	☐ Lemon

AMERICAN BREAKFAST 450
Juice:	☐ Watermelon	☐ Orange	☐ Pineapple
	☐ Tomato	☐ Grapefruit	☐ Carrot
Bread:	☐ Muffins	☐ Toasted Bread	☐ Bagel
	☐ Danish Pastries	☐ Croissants	☐ Multigrain
Eggs:	☐ Fried	☐ Scrambled	☐ Poached
	☐ Boiled (minutes)		
	With ☐ Sausage	☐ Ham	☐ Bacon
Beverage:	☐ Coffee	☐ Decaffeinated Coffee ☐ Tea	☐ Milk
	With ☐ Sugar	☐ Cream ☐ Milk	☑ Lemon

Guest's signature _____

All prices are in NT dollars and subject to
10% service charge.

CHAPTER 11

You will hear three guests phoning to order breakfast in their rooms. Listen and note down.

(a) what the guest in Room 123 wants by ticking (∨) breakfast menu.

(b) what the guests in Room 269 and 336 want on this form?

Room Service	Time Required	Breakfast Order
269		
336		

CONVERSATION

Jessica Kelly has just got to her room at the hotel, after her trip to Washington D.C.. It's 11:30 p.m. She didn't eat anything on the flight, so she's decided to order something from room service.

Jessica: Press nine ... right.

Room service: This is room service. Bob speaking.

Jessica: Good evening. This is room 903. I'd like to order something to eat.

Room service: Right. Excuse me. Ms. Kelly?

餐飲英語

Jessica: That's right.

Room service: What can I get for you?

Jessica: OK. I'll have a mixed lettuce salad, please.

Room service: Will that be with Thousand Is ...?

Jessica: Just oil and vinegar, please.

Room service: Anything else?

Jessica: Mmm. I'd like a beef stew with curry sauce, and a glass of sweet white wine, please.

Room service: There're two small bottles of white wine in the mini-bar, Ms. Kelly.

Jessica: I know, but I don't care for the brand. I'll take a glass of the California Chardonnay, please.

Room service: OK.

Jessica: How long will it be?

Room service: We're not that busy right now. It'll be with you in about twenty minutes.

Jessica: That's great. Thank you.

USEFUL EXPRESSIONS

1. Good morning/afternoon/evening room service.
   早安／午安／晚安，客房餐飲服務。

2. Breakfast is available from 6:00 a.m. to 11:00 a.m.

   早餐的供應時間是從早上六點到十一點。

3. You'll find the menu for room service in the stationery folder in your room.

   您在房間的文具夾裡可以找到客房服務的菜單。

4. At what time shall we serve it?

   您要我們什麼時間送過去？

5. It should take about thirty minutes, sir.

   大約需要三十分鐘。

6. I'll have your dinner sent up to you as soon as possible, sir.

   我會儘快派人將您的晚餐送上去。

7. Your order should be there in about fifteen minutes.

   您點的東西大約十五分鐘左右會送過去。

8. May I have your room number, please?

   請問您的房間號碼是幾號？

9. This is room service. May I come in?

   客房服務，我可以進來嗎？

10. May I place the trolley/tray here?

    我可以把餐車／餐盤放在這裡嗎？

11. Where should I put the trolley/tray?

請問要我把餐車／餐盤放在哪裡？

12. When you have finished, and wish to have your trolley/ tray removed, please dial number 8 for room service. We'll send someone to collect your trolley/tray. Or you may leave the trolley/tray on the hallway.

如果您用好餐點，請撥8到餐飲服務部，我們會派人來將您的餐車／餐盤收走。或者您也可以將餐車／餐盤放置在門口走道旁。

13. Could you sign the bill, please?

請您簽一下帳單好嗎？

PAIR WORKS

Knight Castle Inn   Room Service

Available 24 hours a day. Press 9

～SANDWICHES～

Knight Castle Club Sandwich $195

Layers of ham, chicken, egg, bacon, lettuce, tomato and mayonnaise.

Giant Croissant Sandwich $160

Scrambled eggs with smoked salmon and spring onion accompanied by fresh fruits

Hamburger and French Fries $155

12 oz American beef, onions, tomato, ketchup with choice of egg, cheese or

bacon served with French fries

～SALADS～

Chef's Salad $230

Chicken, ham, beef, olive, avocado served on a bed of crispy lettuce.

Choice of six dressings - Thousand Island, Blue Cheese, French, Italian, Yogurt.

Freshly Grilled Tuna "Nicoise" $190

Tuna, anchoivies, green beans, olives, egg, capers served on bed of lettuce

Choice of dressings as above.

～o O o～

Chef's Vegeetarian Special $150

Stir-fried seasonable vegetables in soy sauce, served with tofu.

Children's Specials   All $200 each

Pizza

Spaghetti with meatball sauce

Child's burger and fries

餐飲英語

Look at the above menu. In pairs, order a room service meal for:

(a) a family with two children

(b) someone who wants a large meal

(c) a vegetarian

(d) yourself

VOCABULARY & PHRASES:

<u>Nouns</u>

stationery folder   trolley

<u>Verb</u>

require

TAPESCRIPT

TAPESCRIPT

CONVERSATION

CHAPTER 1

Listening I

1. Customer: Good afternoon. I'd like to book a table for three for tomorrow night at a quarter after six. My name's Lisa Liu. Would it be possible for us to sit near the window?

   Host: Certainly, madam.

2. Customer: Hello! I want to have a table for six on August 9th at about half-past-eight pm. I'm Paul Wang.

   Hostess: I'm sorry, sir. We're fully booked at eight-thirty on August 9th. But we could seat you at seven-

餐飲英語

thirty.

  Customer: All right. That'll be fine.

3. Customer: Good evening. I'd like to reserve a table for eight for lunch on Friday. We'll get to the restaurant at about eleven. This is Jerry Wu. One member of my party is a vegetarian. Do you have any meals suitable for him?

  Hostess: Sure, we do.

Listening II

A.

1. Customer: I have a reservation for eight on Tuesday. But we want to come on Saturday rather than Tuesday.

2. Customer: We originally reserved a table for three. But now there will be two extra people.

3. Customer: We've booked a table for tonight at six fifteen. But we want to postpone it until seven. Is that OK?

4. Customer: I'm afraid I've got to cancel my booking. That's for lunch at one.

5. Customer: We'd like to sit in the private room instead of by the window.

B.

1. Customer: I've a reservation for eight on Tuesday. But we want to come on Saturday rather than Tuesday.

   Hostess: I'm sorry, sir. We're fully booked on Saturday.

2. Customer: We originally reserved a table for three. But now there will be two extra people.

   Host: Yes, madam. That would be fine.

3. Customer: We've booked a table for tonight at six-fifteen. But we want to postpone it until seven. Is that OK?

   Hostess: I'm very sorry, sir. There are no tables at seven. But you could have a table at five.

4. Customer: I'm afraid I've got to cancel my booking. That's for lunch at one.

   Hostess: Yes, sir. That would be no problem. May I have your name, please?

5. Customer: We'd like to sit in the private room instead of by the window.

   Hostess: Sorry, sir. We've run out of tables in the private

餐飲英語

room.

CHAPTER 2

Listening

A.

1. Customer: Excuse me. What's that thing over there?

   Waitress: It's a coffee pot. It's for holding the coffee.

2. Customer: The sauce boat on my table's missing. Could you bring me one?

   Waiter: Sure. That'll be no problem.

3. Customer: Waiter, what's this spoon for?

   Waiter: It's a dessert spoon, madam. It's for having your dessert.

4. Customer: Can I have another glass? This one is chipped.

   Waiter: Yes, madam. I'll get you one right away.

5. Customer: Could you bring me another knife? This one's blunt.

   Waitress: I'm sorry, sir. I'll bring one for you immediately.

B.

Amy: I broke a glass!

Mother: Oh, no! Excuse me, waiter. Could you help us?

Waiter: Certainly, but I'll be back in a minute.

Mother: What a mess! Let's clean up this water.

Father: Can you hand me some napkins?

Mother: Sure. Here.

Waiter: OK, ma'am. Let me get this broken glass.

Mother: Thank you. We really appreciate it.

Waiter: No problem.

CHAPTER 3

Listening

A.

1. Man: What kind of dressing would you like?

2. Woman: What would you like for dessert?

3. Man: Could I have a table for six, please?

4. Woman: How do you like your steak?

5. Man: Can I get you anything to drink?

6. Woman: Are you ready to order?

B.

1. Waiter: Are you ready to order?

Woman: Yes. I'd like the spaghetti with meatballs.

2. Waitress: Anything for you to drink, sir?

   Man: Yes. Beer, please.

3. Woman: Waiter?

   Waiter: Yes, ma'am?

   Woman: Could you bring us some more coffee?

   Waiter: Just a minute.

4. Man: I'll have the lamb chops.

   Waitress: With mashed potato or baked potato?

   Man: Mashed potato, please.

5. Waitress: Would you like soup with that?

   Man: No. I'll just have a salad and tea.

6. Waitress: May I take your order now?

   Man: Not yet. We need a little more time.

   Waitress: OK. I'll come back.

C.

Waitress: Can I get you anything to drink?

Tony: Yes, We'll have jasmine tea, please.

Waitress: Are you ready to order?

Amy: I'll have the vegetable soup to start.

Waitress: Vegetable soup, yes. And for you, sir?

Tony: I'll take the barbecued suckling pig.

Waitress: I'm sorry. We don't have any barbecued suckling pig, sir.

Tony: But it says here ....

Waitress: Sorry, but we are out of suckling pig.

Tony: OK. Then I'll have the drunken chicken.

Waitress: Drunken chicken. And to follow?

Amy: Which one is spicier? Kungpao chicken or braised beef with chili?

Waitress: Kungpao chicken is spicier than the braised beef with chili.

Amy: Then I'll take the kungpao chicken. I like spicy food.

Tony: And I'll try the fried rice with salmon.

Waitress: Would you like some dessert?

Amy: I'll have mango pudding, please.

Tony: I'll pass.

Waitress: All right. Thank you.

CHAPTER 4

Listening I

Woman 1: I love to eat this at the movies. Sometimes I even make it myself at home. It's really easy. First, you put a little oil in a pan. Then heat the oil. When the oil's hot—but not too hot—put in the kernels. Next, when you see they're starting to pop, cover the pan. Shake the pan a little until the noise stops. After that, pour it into a bowl. Finally, sprinkle a little salt over it and enjoy.

Man 1: Let me tell you how to make a dish that I'm good at cooking. First, chop the bacon, onion, and green pepper. Then, put bacon in the pan with some oil. Add the onion and green pepper. After that, mix rice with the bacon, onion, and pepper. Beat some eggs add rice, cook five minutes. Finally, add soy sauce. Serve with tomato and cucumber.

Woman 2: First, mix the scallions, celery, and fennel in a large bowl. Add the dressing and toss well.

Then, cut the cucumber into thin slices. Tear all the mixed leaves into manageable-sized pieces. After that, add salt and pepper. Cover and chill for up to two hours. Toss before serving.

Man 2: Some people eat the frozen kind from the supermarket, but I like to make my own. You need dough, olive oil, sauce, and cheese — lots of cheese. First, you roll out the dough into a circle and rub a little oil on it. Then put the dough into your oven and bake for a few minutes. Next, spoon a little sauce over the dough. After that, cover the sauce with grated cheese. Then put it back into the oven and bake for another ten minutes or until the cheese melts. Finally, cut it into slices. You'll love it.

Listening II

Person 1

Interviewer: What's one of your favorite dishes?

Man: Hmm. One of my favorite dishes is sukiyaki.

Interviewer: Sukiyaki?

餐飲英語

Man: Yes, sukiyaki.

Interviewer: Is that a Japanese dish?

Man: Yes, it's a popular dish in Japan.

Interviewer: What exactly is sukiyaki?

Man: Well, everything is cooked together in one pot.

Interviewer: Oh, I see. Umm ... what's it made of?

Man: Well, usually it's made of beef and vegetables and
    noodles.

Interviewer: How's it cooked?

Man: It's simmered. The meat and vegetables and noodles
    are cooked together in a special hot broth.

Interviewer: Like a soup?

Man: Right.

Interviewer: Sounds good. What does it taste like?

Man: It's actually a little sweet.

Interviewer: Sweet?

Man: Yeah. That's because the hot broth is a little sweet.

Interviewer: Oh. Well, thanks. I'll have to try it sometime.

Man: Yes, do. I think you'll like it.

Person 2

Interviewer: What's one of your favorite dishes?

Man: What's one of my favorite dishes? Well, I guess I'd have to say tagliatelle Bolognese.

Interviewer: Umm, what's that?

Man: It's a traditional Italian dish. It's a kind of pasta.

Interviewer: Pasta?

Man: Yeah.

Interviewer: Hmm. What's it made of?

Man: Well, it's topped with a rich, meaty sauce based on ground beef and a chopped mixture of celery, onion, carrot and garlic.

Interviewer: How's it cooked?

Man: Everything's put into a big pot and boiled for one hour.

Interviewer: So, what does it taste like?

Man: It's delicious. You should try it sometime.

Interviewer: Mmm.

Person 3

Interviewer: What's one of your favorite dishes?

Man: One of my favorite dishes. Hmm. Well, I love mango souffle.

Interviewer: Mango souffle? What's that?

Man: It's a dessert.

餐飲英語

Interviewer: You mean it's sweet?

Man: Kind of. It's sweet but not really sweet like most desserts.

Interviewer: No?

Man: No. That's why I like it.

Interviewer: So, what's it made of?

Man: Oh, let's see. Mostly egg yolk, whipped cream, and mango.

Interviewer: and how's it cooked?

Man: You don't have to cook it. After you finish making it, you chill it for up to two hours. And then it's served cold.

Interviewer: Sounds good. I'll have to try it.

CHAPTER 5

Listening I

A.

Interviewer: What's a good restaurant in Taipei?

Vivian: Well, there's a place I just love called Sakura.

Interviewer: Sakura? That sounds Japanese.

Vivian: Yeah, it is. Do you like Japanese food?

Interviewer: Mmm, yeah. I love sushi.

Vivian: Oh, then you have to go to Sakura. Their sushi is out of this world. In fact, you should sit at the sushi bar so you can watch the chef making the sushi.

Interviewer: Wow.

Vivian: Yeah. It's a pretty fancy place, actually.

Interviewer: Sounds fancy.

Vivian: I love it. What can I say? The food is delicious and the service is excellent. Everyone there is very polite and helpful.

Interviewer: And how are the prices?

Vivian: Oh, well, it's expensive. Really expensive. It'll cost you almost three thousand dollars for two people, but believe me it's worth it. I think it's the best restaurant in town.

B.

Interviewer: What's a good restaurant in Taipei?

Jim: Well, I'd recommend a place I know called the Fisherman's House.

Interviewer: The Fisherman's House ... I'll bet it serves

seafood, right?

Jim: Good guess. As a matter of fact the Fisherman's House was voted the best seafood restaurant in Taipei.

Interviewer: Really. So, what's it like?

Jim: It's very nice. It's in a big house by Green Park. It's really kind of romantic.

Interviewer: Yeah?

Jim: Oh, yeah. It's the perfect place for the perfect evening. It's the kind of place you go to with someone special.

Interviewer: I see. And how's the service? It must be pretty good.

Jim: Oh, the service is great. The waiters are very good. Quick yet polite.

Interviewer: How are the prices?

Jim: It's a little expensive, but not too bad.

C.

Interviewer: What's a good restaurant in Taipei?

Sophie: A good restaurant—Well, I like to take my friends to a place called Corner Cafe.

Interviewer: Corner Cafe? Now that's an interesting name. What kind of food does it serve?

TAPESCRIPT

Sophie: Oh, regular north American. You know, burgers, pastas, sandwiches. But I especially like the tuna fish croissant there. It's really tasty.

Interviewer: Oh, I see. So what's it like?

Sophie: Corner Cafe? Well, it's small—so it's always crowded. But it's really a fun place. Very informal and friendly.

Interviewer: What do you mean?

Sophie: Well, for example, during the weekend, there're always lots of people outside waiting to get in.

Interviewer: Uh-huh.

Sophie: So, Kenny—the owner of the place—will go outside and serve everyone a free drink.

Interviewer: Wow, that's nice.

Sophie: Yeah. That's the kind of place it is. Everyone there is super friendly.

Interviewer: And how are the prices?

Sophie: Cheap. It's a great deal.

Listening II

1. Woman: Excuse me.

Waiter: Yes, madam.

Woman: This napkin's stained. And I asked someone to bring me another one ten minutes ago. But no one did.

Waiter: I'm sorry, madam. I'll bring you one immediately.

2. Woman: How was the restaurant you had dinner at last week?

Man: It was very good. The food was delicious and the prices were average.

3. Woman: Did you enjoy it?

Man: Well, the tea was cold and the pork was a little tough. I think it was overcooked.

4. Waitress: Is everything all right, sir?

Man: Yes. I'm enjoying the oysters.

5. Woman: Waiter.

Waiter: Yes, madam.

Woman: There's a hair in my soup.

Waiter: I'm very sorry, madam. I'll bring you some other soup right away.

TAPESCRIPT

CHAPTER 6

Listening I

Man: And now here's Ann Poly, our food reporter.

Woman: Good morning. I'm here today with three people from different cities around the world. We're gonna talk about what foods are popular in their cities. Our first question is for Yama Kato from Tokyo. Mr. Kato, what's the most popular kind of food in Tokyo?

Japanese man: Well, Japanese food is the most popular. But then I think the second most popular is Chinese. Then, French.

Woman: So, in your opinion, Japanese food is first, Chinese food is second, and French food is third.

Japanese man: Yes, I think so.

Woman: OK, thank you. Now for Diana Foster from London. What's the most popular kind of food in London, Ms. Foster?

English woman: French food is the most popular in London.

餐飲英語

After French is Italian, then Chinese.

Woman: So French food is the most popular in London, followed by Italian and then Chinese. What about in New York? We have Robert Ford to tell us about popular foods in New York.

New York man: Well, we have so many people from so many places in New York. It's hard to say, but I think American is first, Italian is second, and French is third.

Woman: So in New York most people go to American, Italian, or French restaurants. Talking about all these wonderful foods is making me hungry. Let's go have lunch.

Listening II

Dear Brenda,

Mom called last night. She told me you're going to Los Angeles next month. You know, I was there last year and it was great—especially the food. Here are three or four restaurants you must go to. First, there's a wonderful Chinese restaurant in Chinatown. It's called the Great Wall.

The food is fabulous and it's really inexpensive. Try the steamed shrimp with garlic. It's delicious. There's a good Italian restaurant, Olive Garden, on California Street. They have great pizza and dessert. The Buena Vista is a terrific Mexican restaurant near Sunset Boulevard. Try the tortillas. Finally, there's an excellent Japanese restaurant in the Daytona Center, called Ishizen. It's a little expensive, but the sushi and sukiyaki are delicious.

Have fun and send me a postcard.

CHAPTER 7

Listening

A.

Barmaid: Good evening, sir. What would you like?

Customer: What kinds of whisky have you got?

Barmaid: We've got our own brand, sir. Or I can give you an Irish whisky, a rye, a bourbon or a malt.

Customer: I'll have an Irish. A double, please.

Barmaid: Certainly, sir. Would you like any water or ice with it?

餐飲英語

Customer: No water, thank you. That spoils it. I'll have just ice.

Barmaid: Certainly, sir.

B.

Barman: Good evening, madam. Can I get you something to drink?

Customer: Yes. Can you bring us one draft beer, a gin, and a cocktail.

Barman: How would you like your gin?

Customer: Oh, let me see. Tonic, please.

Barman: A gin and tonic. Would you like ice and lime with it?

Customer: Yes, please.

C.

Barmaid: Good evening. What can I get for you?

Customer 1: What about you, Peter?

Customer 2: Cognac for me. Let's look at the tariff here. Oh, not a cognac. I'll have the ormagnac.

Customer 1: And you, Mathew?

Customer 3: A brandy. Just as it comes, no ice or anything.

Customer 1: And I'll have a Perrier.

Barmaid: Certainly, sir. That's an armagnac, a brandy, and a Perrier. There's ice on the bar there, if you want any.

Customer 3: OK.

CHAPTER 8

Listening

Waitress: Are you ready to order?

Woman: Yes. She'd like a grilled chicken sandwich and French fries. He'd like a roast beef sandwich, and I'd like a grilled cheese sandwich and a small diet coke.

Waitress: OK, a grilled chicken sandwich and fries for the girl, a roast beef sandwich for the boy, and the grilled cheese sandwich and diet coke is for you.

Woman: That's right.

Girl: Mom, can I have a chocolate milk shake, too? Please.

Boy: Me, too. I want a strawberry milk shake, please.

Woman: OK, ok. One chocolate and one strawberry milk shake, please.

Waitress: OK. And for you, sir?

Man: I'd like a bacon, lettuce, and tomato sandwich.

Waitress: OK. That's a BLT and a cup of hot soup. What would you like to drink?

Man: A hot coffee. And afterward, we'll all have apple pie.

Waitress: So that's one diet coke, one strawberry milk shake, one chocolate milk shake, one hot coffee, and four pieces of apple pie.

Man: That's right.

CHAPTER 9

Listening

A.

First customer: I'd like to use my American Express card, if that's OK.

Waitress: Certainly, sir. That'll be fine.

B.

Second customer: I've got a whole lot of your currency I want to use up, so I think I'll pay with that.

Waiter: Certainly, madam.

C.

Third customer: Are these traveller's checks OK with you ?

Waiter: What currency are they, madam?

Third customer: Japanese yen.

Waiter: I'm very sorry, madam. We only accept traveller's checks in US dollars.

Third customer: Oh, well, then I'd better use the cash I've got left.

D.

Fourth customer: Hmm. Can I pay by check?

Waitress: I'm sorry, sir. We don't accept personal checks. Do you have an international credit card?

E.

Fifth customer: Can I use these French francs? You see, I've got very few marks left.

Waitress: I'm not sure, sir. I'll just have to ask the cashier.

F.

Sixth customer: I don't have any NT dollars. Is it OK if I pay in US dollars?

Waitress: Certainly, sir.

CHAPTER 10

Listening I

Man: Here's a typical Japanese breakfast.

Woman: Mmm, it looks good — soup, fish, pickles, rice, tea, and ... what's that? In the red box.

Man: Seaweed.

Woman: Seaweed? They eat seaweed in Japan?

Man: Uh-huh. It's good for you. Here, try some.

Woman: What do people usually have for breakfast in China?

Man: Well, they have congee with a lot of side dishes.

Woman: Congee? What's that?

Man: It's rice soup.

Woman: Rice soup, huh? Is it good?

Man: Uh-huh.

Woman: What else do they have for breakfast in China?

Man: Well, with the congee they usually have pickled cucumber, salted egg, dried pork, and beancurd.

Woman: Wow. That's a lot.

TAPESCRIPT

Man: Bacon and eggs, toast and butter, orange juice, coffee. Do people in the United States always have such big breakfasts?

Woman: No, a lot of Americans watch their weight. They just have a small breakfast, or no breakfast at all.

Man: Really? I'd rather have a big American breakfast any day.

Woman: Is that a typical English breakfast?

Man: Yes, it is. Fried eggs with ham, sausage, grilled tomatoes, and mushrooms. And of course toast and jam, and tea with milk.

Woman: Tea with milk, huh? I always have tea with lemon.

Man: You should try it with milk and a little sugar. It's delicious.

Listening II

A.

Waitress: Which breakfast would you like, sir?

Guest 1: Oh, I'll have the Japanese breakfast, I think.

B.

Guest 2: I'd like the Continental breakfast, please.

餐飲英語

Waiter: Yes, certainly, madam.

Guest 2: With orange juice.

Waiter: And what kind of cereal would you like?

Guest 2: Corn flakes.

C.

Waiter: How would you like your egg done?

Guest 3: Boiled, please.

Waiter: For how many minutes shall we boil your eggs?

Guest 3: For three minutes.

D.

Waitress: Good morning, sir. Are you ready to order?

Guest 4: Yes, thanks. I'll have the cinnamon raisin bagel and
a cup of coffee.

Waitress: Regular or decaffeinated?

Guest 4: Decaffeinated, please.

E.

Waitress: Would you like something to drink?

Guest 5: Yes, I'll have a hot chocolate, and one omelet with
tomatoes, mushrooms, and cheese, please.

F.

Waiter: Good morning, madam. Here's our breakfast menu.

Guest 6: I'd like a healthy breakfast. Let me see, yes, I'll have the fruit salad, multigrain and decaffeinated coffee. That'll do me nicely.

CHAPTER 11

Listening

A.

Waitress: Good morning, room service.

Guest: Hello, this is Darby Smith in room 123. Can I have breakfast in my room, please?

Waitress: Certainly, Mr. Smith, what would you like to have?

Guest: Well, can I have one American breakfast with carrot juice, scrambled eggs with bacon, a Danish pastry and decaffeinated coffee and one continental breakfast with grapefruit juice, natural yogurt, muffins and tea with milk.

Waitress: Right, thank you, Mr. Smith. So that's one American breakfast with carrot juice ....

B.

Waiter: Good evening, room service.

Guest: Good evening. Can I order breakfast for tomorrow morning, please?

Waiter: Certainly, madam. Could I have your name and room number, please?

Guest: My name's Mrs. Ford and it's room 269.

Waiter: 269, right, Mrs. Ford. Now what time would you like your breakfast served?

Guest: At quarter to seven.

Waiter: And what would you like?

Guest: Two continental breakfasts, both with tomato juice and natural yogurts. One with black coffee and one with tea with lemon.

Waiter: Two continental breakfasts with tomato juice, and natural yogurt. One with black Coffee, and one with tea with lemon.

Guest: Right.

Waiter: What would you like for the bread?

Guest: One croissant and one wholewheat roll.

Waiter: Would you like a morning newspaper, too?

Guest: Oh, yes, please.

Waiter: Well, thank you very much, madam. Good night,

TAPESCRIPT

Mrs. Ford.

Guest: Good night, thank you.

C.

Waitress: Good evening, room service.

Guest: Oh, this is Mr. Brown, room 336. Can I order breakfast for tomorrow, please?

Waitress: Certainly, sir. What time would you like your breakfast served?

Guest: Er ... quarter past eight.

Waitress: And what would you like?

Guest: I'd like a Taiwanese breakfast with jasmine tea.

Waitress: Is that just one breakfast?

Guest: Yes, please.

Waitress: So that's one Taiwanese breakfast with jasmine tea.

Guest: Right.

Waitress: Would you like a morning newspaper too, sir?

Guest: Oh, yes. Do you have any English language newspaper?

Waitress: Yes, we do. We have the China Post. Well, thank you very much, Mr. Brown, good night.

Guest: Good night.

VOCABULARY & PHRASES

CHAPTER 1

<u>Nouns</u>

customer〔'kʌstəmə〕顧客

host/hostess〔host〕〔'hostɪs〕領檯

Valentine's Day〔'væləntaɪns〕情人節

band〔bænd〕樂團

request〔rɪ'kwɛst〕要求

table chart〔tʃɑrt〕座位表

reservation chart〔rɛzə'veʃn〕預訂表

children's menu〔'mɛnju〕兒童菜單

<u>Verbs</u>

to reserve〔rɪ'zɝv〕預訂

to book 預訂

to confirm〔kən'fɝm〕確認

to cancel〔'kænsḷ〕取消

to postpone〔post'pon〕延期

to put ... forward to〔'fɔrwəd〕提前

TAPESCRIPT

to look forward to 期待……

<u>Adjectives</u>

available〔əˋveləbļ〕可資利用的

be fully booked〔ˋfulɪ〕全都被訂滿了

<u>Prepositions</u>

be run out of ... 沒有……

CHAPTER 2

<u>Nouns</u>

waiter/waitress〔ˋwetɚ〕〔ˋwetrɪs〕服務人員

table setting〔ˋsɛtɪŋ〕餐桌擺設

tableware 餐具

soy sauce〔sɔɪ〕〔sɔs〕醬油

Shao Shin wine 紹興酒

<u>Chinaware</u> 瓷器

show plate〔plet〕展示盤

dinner plate 大餐盤

bread & butter plate 麵包＆奶油碟

tea cup & saucer〔ˋsɔsɚ〕茶杯＆底盤

Sauce boat 佐料盅

Creamer〔ˋkrimɚ〕奶盅

Sugar bowl〔bol〕糖盅

Toothpick holder〔tuθ,pɪk〕〔ʹholdɚ〕牙籤盅

Ashtray〔ʹæʃ,tre〕煙灰缸

Glassware 玻璃器皿

water goblet〔ʹɡɑblɪt〕水杯

wine glass 酒杯

liqueur glass〔lɪʹkɜ〕香甜酒杯

Shao Shin serving glass 紹興公杯

champagne tulip〔ʃæmʹpen〕〔ʹt(j)uləp〕香檳杯

Irish coffee glass〔ʹaɪrɪʃ〕愛爾蘭咖啡杯

punch bowl〔pʌntʃ〕雞尾酒缸

shot glass〔ʃɑt〕純酒杯

sherry & port glass 雪莉酒／波特酒杯

Silverware, Cutlery〔ʹsɪlvɚ,wɛr〕〔ʹkʌtlərɪ〕銀器

dinner fork & knife 大餐叉＆餐刀

salad fork & knife 沙拉叉＆沙拉刀

dessert fork & spoon 點心叉＆點心匙

fish knife & fork 魚刀＆魚叉

butter knife 奶油

chopstick stand 筷架

tea/coffee spoon 茶／咖啡匙

soup ladle〔ˈledl̩〕湯杓

cake server〔ˈsɝvɚ〕蛋糕鏟

Other Items

soup tureen〔tjuˈrin〕湯鍋

napkin〔ˈnæpkɪn〕口布

towel〔ˈtaʊəl〕毛巾

toothpick 牙籤

corkscrew〔kɔɚk͵skru〕開瓶器

salt & pepper shakers〔ˈʃekɚ〕鹽＆胡椒罐

chopsticks〔tʃɑp͵stɪks〕筷子

water jug〔dʒʌg〕水壺

wine cooler 冰酒桶

coffee/tea pot〔pɑt〕咖啡／茶壺

finger bowl 洗手盅

tray〔tre〕托盤

tablecloth〔ˈtebl̩͵klɔθ〕桌布

chafing dish〔ˈtʃefɪn〕保溫熱鍋

bill holder〔ˈholdɚ〕帳單夾

service towel 服務巾

Verbs

to cut 切割

to hold〔hold〕裝

to break 打開

to get out ... 把……取出

to keep ... cool 保持……冰冷

<u>Adjectives</u>

stained〔stend〕有污點的

broken 破的

chipped〔tʃɪpd〕有裂痕的

blunt〔blʌnt〕鈍的

bent〔bɛnt〕彎曲的

dirty 髒的

<u>Prepositions</u>

on the top 在上面

on the bottom〔tɑtəm〕在底下

on the left 在左邊

on the right 在右邊

right away 立刻

TAPESCRIPT

CHAPTER 3

<u>Nouns</u>

clam chowder〔klæm〕〔ˈtʃaudɚ〕蛤蜊巧達湯

pork rib〔rɪb〕豬肋排

(peach) pie（水蜜桃）派

(turkey) sandwich（火雞）三明治

fried chicken 炸雞

(Thousand Island) dressing〔ˈdrɛsɪŋ〕（千島）沙拉醬

(smoked) salmon〔ˈsæmən〕（煙燻）鮭魚

sirloin steak〔ˈsɝlɔɪn〕沙朗牛排

appetizer/hors d'oeuvre〔ˈæpəˌtaɪzɚ〕〔ɔɚˈdɝv〕開胃菜

onion soup 洋蔥湯

main course/entree〔ˈɑntre〕主菜

caviar〔ˌkævɪˈɑr〕魚子醬

oyster sauce〔ˈɔɪstɚ〕〔sɔs〕蠔油

scallop〔ˈskɑləp〕干貝

gingko〔ˈgɪŋko〕百果

bamboo〔bæmˈbu〕竹筍

tenderloin steak〔ˈtɛndɚˌlɔɪn〕菲力牛排

tartare sauce〔ˈtɑrtɚ〕塔塔醬

餐飲英語

mayonnaise〔meə'nez〕美奶滋（蛋黃醬）

ketchup〔'kɛtʃəp〕番茄醬

horseradish sauce〔hɔrs,rædıʃ〕辣根醬（芥末醬）

abalone〔æbə'lonı〕鮑魚

chili sauce〔'tʃılı〕辣椒醬

tabasco sauce〔tə'bæsko〕辣醬油

baby chicken 春雞

consomme〔,kɑnsə'me〕清燉肉湯

mashed potato〔mæʃd〕馬鈴薯尼

celery〔'sɛlərı〕芹菜

Beaujolais 薄酒來酒

lobster gratin〔'grætṇ〕焗烤龍蝦

chocolate sundae〔'sʌndı〕巧克力聖代

dessert〔dı'zɜt〕點心

beverage〔bɛvərıdʒ〕飲料

(beef) noodles〔'nudḷ〕（牛肉）麵

(rainbow) trout〔traut〕（彩虹）鱒

(black) coffee（黑）咖啡

wheat bread〔hwıt〕全麥麵包

shark's fin〔'ʃɑrk〕〔fın〕魚翅

asparagus〔ə'spærəgəs〕蘆筍

TAPESCRIPT

jellyfish〔ˈdʒɛlɪ‚fɪʃ〕海蜇皮

snail〔snel〕蝸牛

tuna fish〔ˈtunə〕鮪魚

goose liver pate〔pɑˈte〕鵝肝醬

seafood 海鮮

lamb chops〔læm〕〔tʃɑp〕羊排

spaghetti〔spəˈgɛtɪ〕義大利麵

meatball〔ˈmit‚bɔl〕肉丸子

lasagna〔ləˈzɑnjə〕義大利千層麵

(strawberry) mousse〔mus〕（草莓）慕斯

prawn〔prɔn〕大明蝦

eels〔il〕鰻魚

alcohol〔ˈælkə‚hɔl〕酒精

dairy products〔ˈdɛrɪ〕乳製品

fried rice 炒飯

today's special〔ˈspɛʃəl〕今日特餐

cappuccino 義大利奶泡咖啡

earl grey tea〔ɝl〕〔gre〕伯爵茶

tiramisu 義大利乳酪蛋糕

lobster〔ˈlɑbstɚ〕龍蝦

suckling pig〔ˈsʌklɪŋ〕乳豬

rice noodles 米粉

almond〔ˈɑmənd〕杏仁

beancurd〔binkɜd〕豆腐

mango〔ˈmæŋgo〕芒果

coconut〔ˈkokə,nət〕椰子

egg yolk〔jok〕蛋黃

rib eye steak 肋眼牛排

flambe cherries with kirsch〔ˈkɪrʃ〕火焰櫻桃

souffle〔ˈsufle〕酥芙里

(a la carte) menu〔ɑləˈkɑrt〕（單點）菜單

high chair 高腳椅

vegetarian〔vɛdʒəˈtɛrɪən〕素食者

Muslim〔ˈmʌzlɪm〕回教徒

senior citizen〔ˈsinjɚ〕〔ˈsɪtɪzn̩〕老年人

low fat 低脂

low calories〔ˈkælərɪ〕低卡

Jew〔dʒu〕猶太教徒

sea cucumber〔ˈkjukəmbɚ〕海參

pig knuckle〔ˈnʌkl̩〕豬腳

green pepper 青椒

Shao Shin wine 紹興酒

jasmine tea〔ˈdʒæsmɪn〕茉莉花茶

oolong tea 烏龍茶

<u>Verbs</u>

to take an order 點餐

to greet〔grit〕招呼

to take your time 慢慢來

to recommend〔rɛkəˈmɛnd〕推薦

to go with ... 搭配……

to chew〔tʃu〕咀嚼

to digest〔dəˈdʒɛst〕消化

to make up one's mind 決定

to verify〔ˈvɛrəˌfaɪ〕確認

to occupy〔ˈɑkjəˌpaɪ〕佔有

<u>Adjectives</u>

rare（指牛排）稍熟

medium（指牛排）五分熟

well done（指牛排）全熟

pickled〔ˈpɪkl̩d〕用醃汁醃製的

spicy〔ˈspaɪsɪ〕辣的

be suitable for ...〔ˈsutəbl̩〕適合……

light〔laɪt〕清淡的

sour〔'saʊr〕酸的

delicious〔dɪ'lɪʃəs〕美味可口的

excellent〔'ɛkslənt〕很棒的

rich/creamy〔krimɪ〕很濃郁的

be allergic to ...〔ə'lɜdʒɪk〕對……過敏

be on a diet〔'daɪət〕正在節食減肥的

CHAPTER 4

<u>Nouns</u>

Kiwi〔kiwɪ〕奇異果

star fruit 楊桃

honeydew melon〔'hʌnɪ,dju〕〔'mɛlən〕哈密瓜

cauliflower〔'kɔlə,flaʊɚ〕花椰菜

spinach〔'spɪnɪtʃ〕菠菜

parsley〔'pɑrslɪ〕荷蘭芹

basil〔'bæzɪl〕紫蘇；羅勒

rosemary〔roz,mɛrɪ〕迷迭香

mint〔mɪnt〕薄荷

liver〔'lɪvɚ〕肝

kidney〔'kɪdnɪ〕腎

tongue〔tʌŋ〕舌頭

TAPESCRIPT

cuttlefish〔ˈkʌtḷˌfɪʃ〕花枝

sea bass〔bæs〕鱸魚

avocado〔ˌævəˈkɑdo〕酪梨

dumpling〔dʌmplɪŋ〕水餃

eggplant〔ɛgˌplænt〕茄子

tablespoon 湯匙

teaspoon 茶匙

recipe〔ˈrɛsəpɪ〕食譜

ginger〔ˈdʒɪndʒɚ〕薑

vinegar〔ˈvɪnɪgɚ〕醋

olive oil〔ˈɑlɪv〕橄欖油

cod〔kɑd〕鱈魚

mussel〔ˈmʌsḷ〕貽貝

popcorn〔ˈpɑpˌkɔrn〕爆米花

plaice〔ples〕比目魚

breadcrumb〔brɛdkrʌm〕麵包粉

bisque〔bɪsk〕濃湯

sherbet〔ˈʃɝbɪt〕冰沙雪碧

pistachio〔pɪsˈtɑʃɪˌo〕開心果

raisin〔ˈrezn̩〕葡萄乾

peanut〔ˈpiˌnʌt〕花生

Verbs

to grill/broil〔grɪl〕〔ˊbrɔɪl〕在烤架上烤

to steam〔stim〕蒸

to boil〔bɔɪl〕水煮（100℃）

to poach〔potʃ〕水煮（100℃）

to bake 在烤箱中烤

to pour〔por〕倒

to saute〔soˊte〕清油炒

to deep fry 炸

to pan fry 平鍋煎

to roast〔rost〕（指肉類）在烤箱中烤

to stew〔st(j)u〕燉

to fillet〔ˊfɪlɪt〕（指魚、肉）片下來

to chop 剁碎；切斷

to slice〔slaɪs〕切片

to mash 搗碎成泥狀

to dice/cube〔daɪs〕〔kjub〕切丁

to peel〔pil〕剝皮

to stuff〔stʌf〕填塞

to mince〔mɪns〕絞碎

to grate〔gret〕刨絲

TAPESCRIPT

to beat 打

to mix 混合

to marinate〔ˈmærə,net〕浸泡滷汁

to dip〔dɪp〕沾

<u>Adjectives</u>

be garnished with〔ˈgɑrnɪʃd〕隨餐附有⋯⋯

be served with 隨餐搭配有⋯⋯

be accompanied with〔əˈkʌmpənɪd〕隨餐搭配有⋯⋯

be flavored with〔ˈflevəd〕被用⋯⋯來調味

be stuffed with 被填塞滿了⋯⋯

be made from ... 用⋯⋯作成的

be cooked in ...在⋯⋯烹煮

plain/bland〔plen〕〔blænd〕（指食物）清淡的

greasy〔ˈgrizɪ〕油膩的

bitter〔ˈbɪtə〕苦的

CHAPTER 5

<u>Nouns</u>

atmosphere〔ˈætməsfɪr〕氣氛

submarine〔ˈsʌbmə,rin〕潛艇堡

patience〔ˈpeʃəns〕耐心

ambience〔ˈæmbɪəns〕環境；氣氛

guidebook〔ˈgaɪd,buk〕指南

ravioli〔ˌrævɪˈolɪ〕義大利乳酪餃

T-bone steak〔bon〕丁骨牛排

truffle〔ˈtrʌfḷ〕松露

squid〔skwɪd〕烏賊

sign〔saɪn〕招牌

advertisement〔ˌædvɚˈtaɪzmənt〕廣告

parmesan cheese〔ˈpɑrməzæn〕義大利乾酪

crouton〔kruˈtɑn〕麵包丁

praise〔prez〕讚美

complaint〔kəmˈplent〕抱怨

Verbs

to enjoy〔ɪnˈdʒɔɪ〕享用

to apologize〔əˈpɑlə,dʒaɪz〕抱歉

to eat out 外食

to improve〔ɪmˈpruv〕改善

Adjectives

reasonable〔ˈriznəbḷ〕合理的

tender〔ˈtɛndɚ〕柔嫩的

tasty〔testɪ〕美味可口的

TAPESCRIPT

juicy〔'dʒusɪ〕多汁的

tough〔tʌf〕硬的

salty〔'sɔlty〕鹹的

overcooked/overdone 煮過熟的

undercooked/underdone 沒煮熟的

stale〔stel〕（指酒）走味的

tasteless 沒味道的

off（食物）沒味道的

burnt 烤焦的

fresh 新鮮的

ripe〔raɪp〕成熟的

terrible〔'tɛrəbḷ〕可怕的

horrible〔'hɔrəbḷ〕可怕的

awful〔'ɔfʊl〕糟糕的

revolting〔rɪ'voltɪŋ〕令人作嘔的

disappointing〔dɪsə'pɔɪntɪŋ〕令人失望的

average〔'ævəvɪdʒ〕普通的；平常的

flat〔flæt〕（指食物）淡而無味的；（指啤酒等）走了氣的

fishy 有魚腥味的

gracious〔'greʃəs〕親切的

CHAPTER 6

Nouns

map 地圖

sushi 壽司

dim sum 點心

fondue〔ˈfɑndu〕瑞士火鍋

tempura 甜不辣；天婦羅

batter〔bætɚ〕由麵粉、雞蛋等調成的糊狀物

globe fish〔ˈglob‚fɪʃ〕河豚

sake 日本清酒

staple food〔ˈstepḷ〕主食

seaweed〔si‚wid〕海藻；海草

protein〔ˈprotiɪn〕蛋白質

pasta〔ˈpɑstə〕麵食類

steamed egg custard〔ˈkʌstɚd〕蒸蛋

wonton〔ˈwɑn‚tɑn〕餛飩

cholesterol〔kəˈlɛstə‚rol〕膽固醇

stock〔stɑk〕煮肉、骨而得的高湯

soy bean 黃豆

ingredient〔ɪnˈgridɪənt〕成分；材料

TAPESCRIPT

beef carpaccio 義式生牛肉

bouillabaisse〔ˌbuljəˈbes〕馬賽海鮮湯

pheasant〔ˈfɛzn̩t〕雉雞

<u>Verbs</u>

ferment〔ˈfɜmɛnt〕發酵

imitate〔ˈɪməˌtet〕仿效

<u>Adjectives</u>

ethnic food〔ˈɛθnɪk〕各民族的食物

Thai〔taɪ〕泰國的

Japanese 日本的

French 法國的

Greek〔grik〕希臘的

Italian 義大利的

Mexican 墨西哥的

German 德國的

terrific〔təˈrɪfɪk〕很棒的

exotic〔ɛgˈzɑtɪk〕異國風格的

be in the mood for ... 有意……

popular 很受歡迎的

out of this world 非常棒的；超凡的

primary〔ˈpraɪˌmɛrɪ〕主要的

traditional〔trəˈdɪʃənḷ〕傳統的

bonito fish〔bəˈnito〕鰹魚

CHAPTER 7

Nouns

beverage list 飲料單

alcoholic beverage〔ælkəˈhɔlɪk〕酒精性飲料

spirit〔ˈspɪrɪt〕烈酒

iiqueurs〔lɪˈkɜ〕香甜烈酒

(bottled/draft) beer〔dræft〕（瓶裝／生）啤酒

non-alcoholic/soft drinks 非酒精性飲料

root beer 沙士

mineral water〔ˈmɪnərəl〕礦泉水

orange pekoe tea〔ˈpiko〕橘茶

wine list 酒單

champagne 香檳酒

aroma〔əˈromə〕香味

tannin〔ˈtænɪn〕單寧酸

mixture 混合

herbal tea〔ˈ(h)ɜbḷ〕花茶

decaffeinated coffee 低咖啡因飲料

caffeine〔ˈkæfin〕咖啡因

artificial sweetener〔ɑrtəˈfɪʃəl〕代糖

cocktail 雞尾酒

cellar〔ˈsɛləˌ〕酒窖

straight up = with no ice（酒）不加冰塊

on the rocks = with ice（酒）加冰塊

garnish 裝飾物

(orange) slice 柑橘片

straw〔strɔ〕吸管

coaster〔kostəˌ〕杯墊

shaker 搖酒器

instant coffee〔ˈɪnstənt〕即溶咖啡

Adjectives

sparkling〔ˈspɑrklɪŋ〕會冒氣泡的

a variety of〔vəˈraɪətɪ〕各式各樣的

imported〔ɪmˈportɪd〕進口的

domestic〔dəˈmɛstɪk〕國內的

still〔stɪl〕不冒氣泡的

extensive〔ɪkˈstɛnsɪv〕廣泛的；多方面的

tropical〔ˈtrɑpɪkļ〕熱帶的

CHAPTER 8

<u>Nouns</u>

milk shake〔ʃek〕奶昔

chicken nugget〔ʹnʌgɪt〕雞塊

onion ring 洋蔥圈

biscuit〔ʹbɪskɪt〕比司吉麵包

croissant〔krwɑʹsɑn〕可頌牛角

chicken drumstick〔drʌm,stɪk〕雞腿

style pizza 已配好料的比薩

pepperoni 義式香腸

anchovy〔ænʹtʃovɪ〕鯷魚

delivery〔dɪʹlɪvərɪ〕外送

crust〔krʌst〕（比薩的）外皮

crab〔kræb〕螃蟹

<u>Verb</u>

to stand in line〔laɪn〕排隊

TAPESCRIPT

CHAPTER 9

<u>Nouns</u>

bill/check 帳單

credit card 信用卡

company invoice number〔ˈɪnvɔɪs〕統一編號

receipt〔rɪˈsit〕收據

change〔tʃendʒ〕（找回的）零錢

service charge〔tʃɑrdʒ〕服務費

US dollar 美金

Japanese yen〔jɛn〕日幣

foreign currency〔fɑrɪn〕〔ˈkɜ·ənsɪ〕外幣

personal check 個人支票

cashier〔kæˈʃɪr〕櫃檯出納

extra〔ˈɛkstrə〕額外之費用

NT dollar 新臺幣

cover charge（俱樂部、酒吧等處的）服務費；附加費

<u>Verb</u>

charge 收取費用

<u>Adjective</u>

be at someone's discretion〔dɪˈskrɛʃən〕聽憑（某人）決定

CHAPTER 10

<u>Nouns</u>

gluten〔ˈglutn̩〕麵筋

pickled cucumber 醬瓜

dried pork 肉鬆

congee〔ˈkɑndʒi〕稀飯

salted egg 鹹鴨蛋

miso soup 味噌湯

hash brown〔hæʃ〕薯餅

American/continental breakfast〔ˌkɑntəˈnɛntl̩〕美式／歐式早餐

grapefruit〔grep͵frut〕葡萄柚

cereal〔ˈsɪrɪəl〕穀類食品

toast 土司

oatmeal〔ˈot͵mil〕燕麥粥

fig〔fɪg〕無花果

guava〔ˈgwavə〕番石榴

bagel〔ˈbegəl〕猶太培果

multigrain〔ˌmʌltɪgren〕雜糧麵包

marmalade〔ˈmɑrml̩ed〕橘子、檸檬等製成的果醬

TAPESCRIPT

Danish pastries〔ˈdenɪʃ〕〔ˈpestrɪs〕丹麥麵包

doughnut〔ˈdoˌnʌt〕甜甜圈

French toast 法國土司

waffle〔ˈwɑfḷ〕華富餅

pancake〔ˈpænˌkek〕煎餅

muffin〔ˈmʌfɪn〕鬆餅

maple syrup〔ˈmepḷ〕〔ˈsɪrəp〕楓糖漿

preserve〔prɪˈzɜv〕果醬

plain yogurt〔plen〕〔ˈjogət〕原味優酪乳

<u>Adjective</u>

be in a rush〔rʌʃ〕趕時間

CHAPTER 11

<u>Nouns</u>

stationery folder〔steʃənˌɛrɪ〕〔ˈfoldə〕文具夾

trolley〔ˈtrɑlɪ〕推車

<u>Verb</u>

require〔rɪˈkwaɪr〕要求

餐飲英語

餐旅叢書 7

著　　者／蔡淳伊

出 版 者／揚智文化事業股份有限公司

發 行 人／葉忠賢

總 編 輯／孟樊

執行編輯／鄭美珠

登 記 證／局版北市業字第 1117 號

地　　址／台北縣深坑鄉北深路 3 段 260 號 8 樓

電　　話／（02）8662-6826

傳　　真／（02）2664-7633

印　　刷／鼎易印刷事業股份有限公司

初版一刷／2000 年 6 月

初版四刷／2008 年 10 月

ISBN　／957-818-123-X

定　　價／新台幣 400 元

E-mail　／service@ycrc.com.tw

網　　址／http://www.ycrc.com.tw

國家圖書館出版品預行編目資料

餐飲英語 ＝ Restaurant English ／蔡淳伊著.
-- 初版. -- 台北市：揚智文化，2000 [民
89]
　面；　公分. -- （餐旅叢書；7）

ISBN　957-818-123-X（精裝）

1.英國語言 － 讀本

805.18　　　　　　　　　　　89004425